Final Justice

Mystery on Whidbey Island

DAN PEDERSEN

FINAL JUSTICE

DAN PEDERSEN

Final Justice

Mystery on Whidbey Island

Brad Haraldsen Series Book Four

DAN PEDERSEN

Brad Haraldsen Mystery Series

Available from Amazon.com books

Final Deception: *A Whidbey Island Mystery (Book 1)*

Final Passage: *Mystery on the Alaska Ferry (Book 2)*

Final Escape: *Mystery in the Idaho Sawtooths (Book 3)*

Final Justice: *Mystery on Whidbey Island (Book 4)*

Other titles by the Author:

Louis and Fanny: *15 Years on the Alaska Frontier*

Outdoorsy Male: *Short Stories and Essays*

Wild Whidbey: *The Nature of Island Life*

Whidbey Island's Special Places

Cover image Great-horned Owl. c 2018 Dan Pedersen

Email inquiries to Dan Pedersen: *dogwood@whidbey.com*

Copyright © 2018 Dan Pedersen

ISBN: 198684448X
ISBN-13: 978-1986844482

Characters

Brad Haraldsen – retired journalist, NPR contributor, Stanley, Idaho
Irene Haraldsen – Brad's wife, horse rancher and artist, Stanley, Idaho
Bolivar – Brad and Irene's ranch foreman, Stanley, Idaho
Shane Lindstrom – sheriff's detective, Brad's friend, Whidbey Island
Elizabeth Harlowe Lindstrom – Shane's wife, runs Eagles Inn B&B
Judy Lindstrom – Shane's ex-wife, mother of eleven-year-old Billy
Billy Lindstrom – Shane and Judy's son, age eleven
Moose – Billy's dog, a Bichon Frise
Marie Martin – federal wildlife officer, formerly Alaska, now Boise
Robert Yuka – Idaho state trooper, Marie's husband, formerly Alaska
Martin Yuka – Marie and Robert's infant son
Rev. Buford Boh Buckley – supremacist preacher, Whidbey Island
Ida Mae Buckley – Buford Boh's wife
Jerry Buckley – supremacist, Buford Boh's son, Whidbey Island
Raymond Cobb – supremacist sharpshooter, ex-Marine, of Arkansas
Fred Franks – supremacist, bomb maker, from Indiana

Earlier in the Brad Haraldsen Series
Bella Morelli – Brad's first love, murdered, Whidbey Island
Stu Wood – Brad's college roommate and private pilot, suicide
Dakota – Bolivar's daughter, college student, Idaho
Robert Harlowe – Alaska bush pilot, Elizabeth's brother, murdered
Dutch DeGroot – former mayor and real estate developer, Oak Harbor, Washington, in prison
Dorothy DeGroot – former Island County Commissioner, Oak Harbor, Washington, suicide

Foreword

Final Justice is book four in my Northwest mystery series with Idaho journalist Brad Haraldsen and his wife, Irene. Whidbey Island detective Shane Lindstrom is back again, now married to Elizabeth Harlowe, whom he met at the Haraldsen ranch last summer in book three, *Final Escape*. They are joined by their crime-fighting partners, Alaskans Robert Yuka and Marie Martin.

The story and all of its characters are entirely fictional. Some of the inspiration came from actual events on Whidbey Island in the 1980s, mixed with speculation about what could happen in the future if a certain combination of circumstances came about. For some notes about the historical events that inspired this story, see the Afterword on page 175.

For the record, there really was a brothel in Freeland long ago. It has since gone on to a new purpose and I've been to dinner there since its reincarnation. In this story I've changed its name, location and description.

Over the months of writing, several friends helped me tune the story and catch errors. I owe special thanks to Elizabeth Hall and Claire Creighton.

FINAL JUSTICE

Chapter 1

Whidbey Island, December 1984. In the living room of her Lagoon Point home, a woman sits by the crackling warmth of the woodstove, reading. The fire breaks the damp chill of a fall afternoon. Rain patters lightly at the metal roof as daylight ebbs.

The woman loves this quiet season when life turns inward and slows. Days are short and nights are long. Many houses in her shoreline community sit empty in these months when the island sleeps.

The woman opens the door to her stove to add one more log, then closes it and goes to the window to look outside while it's still possible to see. Lights are coming on in the handful of occupied homes, here and there.

She puzzles at the shadows and shapes in her yard. Something seems different and it takes a moment to register:

A man.
In a trench coat.
With a gun.

The man turns and looks right at her. The gun is a rifle with a scope. As she watches, he raises a finger to his lips, signaling her to be silent. He lowers his finger and pulls back his long coat to reveal something shiny clipped to his belt – a badge. The woman nods and backs away from the glass, trembling and suddenly confused. The man continues across the yard in a crouch, carrying his weapon.

Behind him, four more men follow in sheriff's and state patrol uniforms, weapons raised. They wear bulky vests and advance toward a small rental cabin on the sea bluff at the end of the gravel lane.

She's never seen the people who live there, just an occasional light behind curtains.

In the distance, she hears the rhythmic throb of a helicopter growing louder. Moments later the whole yard lights up and the house shakes as the machine passes low and fast, its powerful searchlight sweeping over the house.

The phone rings and it's her husband.

"Honey, I'm stuck on the mainland," he says. "All the ferries are shut down and the bridge is closed. There's some problem on the island – some kind of police action. I can see a Coast Guard cutter . . ."

"I know," the woman says. "There are men in our yard with guns. I think they're surrounding the cabin on the bluff."

"Lock the doors," he says.

Moments later, gunfire begins.

Chapter 2

Summer, the present time. The smoker takes a long draw on his Lucky Strike, holds the smoke for a moment, then coughs and exhales all over the two men across from him.

"Dammit," he says, hacking and coughing some more.

He fixes his eyes on the young man in neatly-creased khakis on the other side of the oak table. The uniformed man wears a black beret with a red swastika.

"She's a problem, Jerry," the smoker says at length in a raspy voice. "*Your* problem. So you dig a hole and make her go away."

He taps the ash from his smoke into a half-full Styrofoam cup of black coffee in front of him, returning his stare to the other man.

Jerry coughs and stares back at him blankly. He scratches his black beard with four fingers and twists his face in an awkward silence.

"For crying out loud, Ray," Swastika man responds at length. "She's my girlfriend. We're not going to bury her in the compound. Christ, this is Mom and Dad's home. We're not doing that."

"Well then you take care of it some other way," Ray says, pounding his index finger at the table.

"She's one of us," Jerry protests.

The third man at the table, professorial and pensive, looks up at Jerry with kind and sympathetic eyes. He adds softly, "She's got no history with us, Jerry. We can't afford that. She's the loose end in all this."

Ray adds, "Keep this girl around and you're going to bring the whole thing crashing down."

"Nothing's going to crash down," Jerry replies. "She's not in a position to do anything."

"She's seen too much," the professorial man says. "You know that."

"Dig a hole," Ray repeats, grinding his cigarette into the table top, "or else I will." He folds his arms across his chest and glares at Jerry, and says no more.

Chapter 3

Elizabeth Lindstrom looks up from the mystery she's reading at a droplet of water swelling larger and larger on the dripper arm of the birdbath. Finally the drop lets go in a staccato blurp of three, splashing to the glass dish and pushing tiny waves outward to the edges. Right away a new drop forms on the arm. The repetition is mesmerizing, Elizabeth's meditation on a summer afternoon.

The owner of Eagles Inn Bed and Breakfast on Whidbey Island brushes a curious bee from her shoulder-length, hazel hair. Her mind drifts as she waits for the rest of her guests. Marie and her baby Martin already are here, napping in the house. Marie's husband, Robert, is out with Elizabeth's husband, Shane. Any time now, their friends Brad and Irene Haraldsen, from Stanley, Idaho, should come up the driveway.

Elizabeth puts her book down.

A solitary Red-breasted Nuthatch drops from the Katsura tree above her and perches atop the dripper arm. It leans forward to study the droplet, checks the surroundings for interlopers, then hops down to the rim to drink.

The bird's mate, which is still on the tree, picks a bug from the bark, holds it in its tiny beak, then shoots from the branch through the opening of a nest box mounted on the side of the inn, setting off a muffled din inside the box.

How does one describe their chatter? It's murmurings, she thinks – subtle and distinct from other birds. She always knows without looking when a family of nuthatches is nearby.

The activity around Elizabeth soothes her – the rituals of courtship, birth and new life in her yard. When she sits quietly, as she does now, the birds lose their fear and settle all around her. While one bird inspects the arm of an Adirondack chair, the next one hops to the dog dish for a drink. Soon, she knows, baby nuthatches will line up alongside their parents on the rim of the bath.

She feels at home here in this refuge from the hectic and crowded mainland. It's the one place where her soul finds peace and renewal.

A few miles away at South Whidbey State Park, the day unfolds differently for Elizabeth's husband, Shane, a county sheriff's detective. In plain clothes, blue jeans and a short-sleeved shirt, the lanky detective pans a video camera across an angry group.

"Keep Whidbey White! Keep Whidbey White!" the group chants as they parade in a circle under a canopy of towering, old growth cedars. Mostly young men, clean cut and collegiate, they carry *White Power!* and *Save Our Homeland* placards under the watchful protection of half-a-dozen overweight men with clubs in paramilitary uniforms and several biker women in leathers, tattooed with Swastikas and skulls on their upper arms.

Sheriff's deputies and state police link arms behind plastic shields to hold back a much larger crowd on the other side of the police line. The counter-demonstrators shout back, "Go home," and "We don't want you."

Several men boost the white-haired Rev. Buford Boh Buckley atop the cargo deck of a flatbed truck and hand him a bullhorn. He takes a moment to stand, teeters off balance briefly, and finds his feet. He smiles and waits politely while the two crowds cheer and taunt each other, then sets his jaw and raises the bullhorn to his mouth. The crowd falls silent.

"Welcome Christian soldiers!"

The protesters erupt into cheers and raise fists in the air. The angular Buckley waits for the commotion to subside before starting to speak.

"Please," he says softly, then finds his voice and speaks with an edge. "Please . . . we don't want any trouble. But if it comes, then let it be the price of liberty. Praise the lord for each and every one of you brave patriots. Stand tall for the sacred white race!" he declares to his followers, eliciting a rousing cheer. "We don't hate Jews, coloreds, Orientals, Muslims or sexual deviants. But the unclean peoples must stay where they belong, and that is not Whidbey Island."

A sharp shout goes up from the parading men as they wave

fists and extend their arms in the Nazi salute.

Toward the back of the crowd, Shane turns to a stocky native in cutoffs and a Hawaiian shirt beside him and remarks, "Not what you expected, are they?"

Robert Yuka, an Idaho state trooper, is visiting on vacation. "I was picturing skinheads," he replies.

"That's the old supremacist image. Everything changed in the last few years with the rise of social media and the hard right turn in the White House."

"Apparently so."

"The skinhead image was putting off too many people. The 2017 violence in Charlottesville, Virginia, is where we really saw the neo-Nazis shift to the all-American look."

"Quite a transformation," Robert says.

"It surprised and shook up a lot of people. Many of the Charlottesville marchers blended right into the crowd – could have been the boy next door, the soldier just back from Afghanistan or the guy who works on the factory floor."

Robert shakes his head. "The window-dressing certainly made it easier for the president to suggest there were very fine people on many sides."

Shane appreciates having Robert with him today. Since the recent election and the radically different tone from the White House, he's found the job of monitoring hate groups and supremacist activity in the community suddenly much harder. Rural counties like this one don't have deep resources to devote to that effort.

"Make sure you pan the whole group as the preacher speaks," Shane says, raising his own camera and snapping a series of close-up photographs. "We'll look at all these images later to identify as many of these people as we can."

Then he adds as an afterthought, "And thanks for helping out today."

"Glad to, Shane. I'd rather be here with you than anywhere else," Robert replies.

One of the supremacist security men fixes a hateful stare on Robert and shouts, "Put away that camera, half breed! Go back to the reservation."

Robert whispers to Shane, "He hasn't met many Alaska

natives."

"Well if he keeps it up, he may soon meet an Idaho State Trooper," Shane chuckles, "now that you've traded your badge in Fairbanks for a new one in Boise."

The Rev. Buford Boh Buckley continues: "We honor the memory today of a fallen soldier who was murdered just a few miles from this spot by cowardly federal agents, working on behalf of the Globalist Conspiracy and New World Order to mongrelize our Sacred White Race."

Shane whispers to Robert, "That was the day the feds sealed off the island and laid siege to some neo-Nazi fugitives who were hiding out in several safe houses. The leader died when his cabin burned down."

"But that's been, what, thirty years?" Robert replies.

"It's fresh in the minds of this crowd. These people believe they are patriots resisting a dark, global conspiracy to take what is rightfully theirs by birth. It ties right into the whole protectionist 'America First' theme."

"And," Robert replies, "It's a short hop from there to closing borders, shutting down international agreements and keeping out people who don't have the right religion, ethnicity or skin color."

"Ethnic cleansing," Shane remarks, looking at the ground. "Not a new idea, just an old one that keeps coming around for another pass."

Chapter 4

Brad Haraldsen turns the Jeep Cherokee up a narrow, tree-lined lane overlooking Holmes Harbor. He and his wife, Irene, are looking forward to this reunion of friends who bonded so closely at their Idaho ranch last summer. It's been a depressing year in some ways and they yearn for the company of good friends. The country is bitterly divided politically and the tone in the land is ugly.

Brad's detective friend, Shane, met his new wife Elizabeth at the Haraldsen ranch and married her shortly after last summer's reunion. Together, Shane and Elizabeth bought the inn here that will be the group's home for the next two weeks. Brad and Irene also look forward to seeing Robert Yuka and Marie Martin on this visit, the Idaho state trooper, formerly of Alaska, and federal wildlife agent who partnered with Brad, Shane and Irene two summers ago on the Alaska Ferry.

Shane and Elizabeth have blocked out the inn exclusively for their friends.

The harbor seems idyllic today. A summer-afternoon breeze ripples the water, and half a dozen sailboats trail from buoys. The tide is out and Brad's eye goes to a Great-blue Heron stalking prey in the shallows. He rounds a bend in the drive and beholds an expanse of lush lawn sloping down from a large, log-style inn. A hammock hangs from two towering fir trees in the front yard. On a lazy afternoon, resting in that hammock, a guy could really lose his sense of time here.

Brad pulls to a stop, windows down, and shuts off the engine. "Isn't this beautiful?" he remarks to Irene. I just want to sit here a moment and inhale."

And now that they're here, he's also thinking about the

agreement he made with Irene for this visit. Can they keep it?

Through the open car window Brad notes the warbling melody of a Black-headed Grosbeak. The grass is emerald green. "Shane and Elizabeth really found themselves a gem in this place."

"It's gorgeous. All the rhododendrons! And those evergreens and ferns," Irene remarks.

Elizabeth and Marie come down the steps to greet them in the driveway, Marie carrying a blanket-wrapped bundle in her arms.

Brad and Irene open their doors, get out and stand. Irene ducks reflexively as a hummingbird zips past her head on its way to a feeder hanging from the porch. Brad straightens up with effort, winces and arches his back to stretch. Elizabeth steps forward, wraps her arms around him and gives him a hug, then repeats the greeting with Irene. Marie, with the bundle in one arm, gives them both a side hug.

"That gray beard is very distinguished on you," Marie remarks. "You look more like Ernest Hemingway every time I see you – minus the drinking and carousing. It's a very writerly look."

"I had to do something to divert attention from my 70-year slide into decrepitude and thinning hair," he laughs.

"Well, you've got the rugged outdoor look with that tan."

"That happens in the intense sunshine of the high plateau."

Brad notices that even as a new mother, the pony-tailed Marie remains tan and fit from her years as a federal wildlife officer in the mountains of Alaska. And she still has the no-nonsense bearing of a law enforcement officer.

Irene has her eye on the baby. "Hurry up and introduce me to the new member of the family," she declares.

Marie hands the bundle to Irene and folds back the cloth on one end. "This is Martin." A tiny pink face looks up at Irene and grins as she cradles the baby's head.

"I love the name," Brad says, "Martin Yuka. You put both your last names together."

"Say hello to your Aunt Irene and Uncle Brad," Marie adds.

The baby coos.

"My kinda guy," Irene says.

"That's Robert's personality. That sweet disposition."

"Speaking of Robert," Brad asks as he opens the tailgate and reaches for a suitcase, "where are Robert and Shane?"

"At a white supremacist rally," Marie replies.

"My god," Brad replies, slapping himself on the face. "I didn't expect that."

Elizabeth interjects. "It's a long story. Come in and get refreshed and then we'll fix you up with a glass of wine and bring you up to speed. The boys should be home pretty soon."

Brad sets down the first suitcase and reaches in for a second one, then follows the women up the steps and into the old lodge. He pauses at the door for another look at the tranquil view of Holmes Harbor and watches a doe and fawn graze contentedly on the lawn. At a nearby birdbath, several Chickadees splash in the water and scold each other.

"This is like a game park," he remarks. "Those deer don't seem the least bit concerned about us."

"They're essentially tame," Elizabeth replies. "We feed them apples."

"I'm afraid in Idaho the deer feed us – with all the hunting, you know."

The lobby is furnished with Oriental rugs and turn-of-the-century antiques, an old Smith-Corona portable typewriter on a roll-top desk, a pump organ, a wall-mounted telephone with a hand crank, and a grandfather clock that suddenly comes to life with two deep chimes: *dong, dong.*

"Half past," Elizabeth declares.

"I feel like we just stepped back in time. Was this place always an inn?"

"No, it started out in the 1800s as a brothel," she replies with a practiced, straight face. "But it's under new management now. Don't worry, we've changed the linens."

"Thank you for that," Irene remarks. "But tell me about the brothel."

"The socialists who founded Freeland thought they needed one, I guess. Imagine you're trying to attract men to live in an isolated place back at the turn of the century. I suppose that's what you did."

Irene nods and Elizabeth continues, "I hope you picked up on the town's name, Free Land. This was one of several socialist communes that sprang up for a little while. There was another in Skagit County called Equality, and some of Freeland's founders came from there."

"Wait till I tell Bolivar I spent my vacation at a brothel," Brad declares with a big smile.

"That's what the husbands all say," Elizabeth replies as she leads them down the hall. She shows Brad and Irene their room, pointing out the bathroom across the hall – which she explains is "updated."

"No pull chain?" Brad asks.

Elizabeth suggests they take a few minutes to get settled and then join Marie and her in the parlor. The baby, Martin, is due for a nap, and Elizabeth's 11-year-old stepson, Billy, is down the road playing with his dog.

Brad smiles, remembering that Billy's dog is a little Bichon Frise with a big galoot's name, Moose.

Brad and Irene unpack a few things, then return to the parlor to find Elizabeth and Marie setting out a vegetable tray, crackers, dip and drinks.

"I feel at home already," Brad remarks.

"That goes for me, as well," Irene agrees.

"Good, because it's your home for the next couple of weeks. Shane and I got the inspiration from your ranch in Stanley."

She adds, "You probably know we fell in love with your place. The minute we got back to Washington we knew we wanted to get married and find something like your ranch where we could have some land and entertain our friends and some paying guests, and raise Billy in a wholesome community. Besides, we're all a little nuts about nature and wildlife, as you know."

It strikes Brad that Elizabeth has grown strong and confident in her new life here with Shane. It's such a contrast from the fear he saw in those eyes a year ago in Idaho, when she was being pursued by a psychopathic boyfriend. That changed after she met Shane.

If any woman can make a pair of plastic-rimmed eyeglasses look downright seductive it's Elizabeth, Brad muses. Something about her reminds him of Meryl Streep. With her love of books, the image of a studious librarian fits her to perfection. Shoulder-length brown hair softens her face. Brad can't get over how naturally she has settled into her dual roles here as a step-mom and innkeeper.

She's come a long way from her sheltered start in life as a meek Jehovah's Witness in the Kent Valley south of Seattle.

*

A few miles away, Ray Cobb lights a Lucky Strike and thinks about his own beginnings and the road that brought him from Arkansas to a compound of militants in the woods of Whidbey Island. As far back as he can remember, pain was the constant in his life – from his mother's disappearance to his father's beatings. It didn't matter what he did right or wrong; he was beaten for it all the same. In any relationship, somebody gives pain and somebody receives it, but pain is the constant, and conflict is the price of survival. Before he leaves this place, he will make somebody else hurt.

He's also painfully aware that Jerry Buckley, who invited him here, isn't up to what needs to be done. Jerry is a pretty boy and an eloquent front man for the supremacist movement, but lacks the backbone for the rougher stuff. More and more he seems a liability to this project.

Backbone is Cobb's department. If he learned nothing in school as a kid, he made up for it in prison. Cobb was behind bars only a few days when he got his first lesson in brotherhood. He was in the shower with several other prisoners when a fight broke out in a nearby cell. Guards came running. Cobb thought at first it had nothing to do with him. But while the guards were over there, fists came at him and he was down in an instant, down on the tile, beaten and bruised, blood flowing down the drain. He made up his mind right then that he'd never again be the one bleeding into the drain.

"Rule one," the medic in the infirmary told him. "Never shower alone – only with friends." He was lucky the attack was nothing serious, the medic told him, "Just a few cracked ribs, a welcome-to-prison initiation."

Cobb exhales a big cloud of smoke from his cigarette. He never thought he needed any friends. But the coloreds had friends, the Latinos had friends.

"You won't survive in here without protection," the medic told him. Cobb thinks this is a lesson his dad should have learned, too. His dad worked his whole life at manual labor and farm jobs alongside colored people who ended up as his bosses. He hated that, and the jobs didn't last. Sooner or later he always got fired for drinking or slacking, or fighting.

The lesson wasn't wasted on the boy; he found his friends in The Aryan Brotherhood.

It was one of the Aryans, the professorial Fred Franks, who explained to Cobb how the coming race war will unfold. The federal government will seize all civilian firearms under a Jewish-authored act of Congress, triggering a patriotic guerilla war by white Aryan groups. As the Jews in government enact ever-more-restrictive laws and oppressive surveillance, a vanguard of Aryan militants will strike back with terrorism, murder and economic sabotage.

As violence between the races escalates, Aryans will seize territory including whole states and military bases, giving them access to sophisticated weaponry and nuclear arms. As a new Civil War breaks out between the separatist states and the liberal federal government, non-whites will flee Aryan territory, speeding the inevitable purification of society.

The entire scenario, Franks explains, is laid out in the *Turner Diaries,* a 1978 novel by William Luther Pierce that has become the supremacist bible for the coming violent revolution against the federal government. The book predicts that the revolution will spread from state to state, going on to sweep the world, finally ending in the eradication of Israel and of non-white racial and religious minorities and gays worldwide.

Cobb plucks the stub of the cigarette from his lips and tosses it on the ground. Then he takes his boot and mashes it into the dirt till the last red sparks wink out.

Chapter 5

At the inn, Brad watches two Douglas Squirrels chatter and chase each other in circles around the trunk of a fir. Their antics are relaxing and entertaining after the disquieting experience they just had on the ferry, not to mention the other disturbing matter that he and Irene have agreed to keep to themselves.

"Is something going on here?" he asks. "There were a lot of state police on the ferry. They singled us out – two 70-year-olds – and asked a lot of questions."

Marie and Elizabeth exchange a knowing look, and Elizabeth nods and purses her lips.

"Your plates," Marie says.

"Plates?"

"The Idaho license plates," Marie says. "Robert and I got the same treatment. There are some undesirable Idaho visitors on the island this week."

As they talk, Brad hears the scrunch of gravel as another vehicle comes up the driveway. He watches out the window as a Chevy Suburban pulls to a stop behind his Cherokee. Shane and Robert get out, both of them carrying cameras.

Shane lopes up the steps and through the door, with Robert on his heels. "You're here!" he declares. "Welcome to the Eagles Inn."

Brad and Irene get up from their wing chairs and hug Shane and Robert.

"Elizabeth and Marie were just telling us you were off with white supremacists today," Brad remarks.

Shane grimaces and shakes his head. "Not where I'd like to be when our best friends are visiting. It's the supremacists' annual rally at the state park to pay tribute to a domestic terrorist who died in a shootout with the feds here three decades ago. These rallies attract some hard cores and we're trying to stay on top of any who may be forming cells to do something illegal."

Brad is curious now. "I recall reading something about that shootout at the time but it's been so long."

"The leader and a group of his followers went on a crime spree in several Western states. Their plan was to trigger a race war and they carried out some robberies to finance it, including an armored car. They also murdered a Jewish talk radio host in Denver. The FBI traced them to several hideouts here on the island and the leader made his last stand here. In fact, the feds burned him out. He died in the fire."

"Now it's coming back to me," Brad says. "I was shocked because it seemed so out of character for Whidbey Island. I still can't imagine those types gaining any traction here."

"They weren't locals," Shane points out. "They were fugitives who came here to lie low. On balance this is an inclusive community of artists, retirees and professionals from all over the country. But we do have a few of the other types, too. Since the new administration took office in Washington, D.C., it's no surprise the supremacists suddenly feel freer to show themselves more and throw their weight around."

Brad shudders, remembering some of these remarks. It's certainly no secret this president has a long history of denigrating people of color. "Why are we having all these people from shithole countries come here?" he asked congressional lawmakers. On another occasion he remarked, "When Mexico sends its people, they're not sending their best. They're bringing drugs. They're bringing crime. They're rapists. And some, I assume are good people."

Remarks like those strike Brad as a national disgrace – unworthy of any president. Aside from the stain on the White House, such remarks knowingly give closet racists implicit permission to persecute minorities and immigrants. To some, separatism now seems an acceptable solution to the nation's problems. The separatists and supremacists want to go back to an earlier time when they held all the power.

Shane brings him back to the moment. "There's something else, too. We have someone on the inside with the neo-Nazis here, an informant, who dropped out of sight several days ago, and I'm starting to worry."

"A cop?"

"No," Shane says. "You're not going to believe who it is. It's complicated for me personally, which is why I asked Robert to help me today."

Chapter 6

"You know how Judy, is," Shane remarks. "My ex is equal parts mother and party girl. If a man's in the room, she's a shameless flirt with a breathless, seductive whisper. When she unleashes that, men can't resist it. She keeps chasing men she finds exciting but who aren't the best marriage material. Big, hairy and sexy – that's her type."

Robert looks at Marie, does a head-fake toward Shane, and shrugs.

Shane glances back and forth between them. "What? You don't think I'm hairy and sexy?"

"Just big," Robert remarks. "Tall like a string bean."

"Hand me a napkin, will you?" Brad asks, and busies himself mopping up the wine he just spilled. The group reclines in Adirondack chairs on the lodge's front porch and shares some cheese and apple slices while sipping their wine. Baby Martin makes goofy faces at Robert from his crib, and Robert makes goofy faces back.

"Isn't he great?" Robert asks. "I think he'll grow up to be a sensitive man like me, rather than a gunslinger like his mom."

"That was the old me," Marie objects. "I'm just a mom now."

Brad nods and smiles. He recalls that as a federal wildlife agent in Alaska, Marie earned instant respect from her male colleagues when she won a gunfight with a poacher and arrested him after he had shot her in the leg. And later, when Robert was wounded, Marie protected him with a hail of return fire till help arrived. Shortly after that they were married.

"I thought maybe after the big fiasco in Idaho last summer Judy would settle down and pull her life together," Brad remarks.

"You might think so," Shane says. "But after she followed me

26

all the way down there and showed up at your ranch and tried to come between Elizabeth and me, she returned to Coupeville and went right back to partying and dating misfits."

"It's her perpetual quest," Robert muses, "searching for someone who will make her feel complete so she can be happy and accept herself as she is. She'll never find it till she learns to love herself first."

Brad remembers the impression Judy made last summer when she showed up uninvited at their ranch, mad as hell, looking for Shane. Robert and Marie were home alone that afternoon while everyone else was away. Here came this buxom, middle-aged woman dressed like a teenager with blond hair, heavy perfume and a short skirt. She was convinced her ex-husband had run away to Idaho with her son and a slut, and she was determined to break it up.

"What is she doing these days?" Marie asks.

"Working as a float nurse at the hospital," Shane replies. "So she works an irregular schedule – whenever they need a nurse to fill in."

"What do you think she wants?" Marie asks.

"Honestly?"

Shane continues, "She wants me back – or thinks she does. But that's not going to happen. I don't know if she'll ever stop trying. Judy is one of those people who wants whatever she can't have."

"So how did you ever wind up with her?"

"My own stupidity. Our history goes back to high school, ok? She's such a flirt, every guy in our class was spellbound by her. She had a thing for me and I was totally smitten by her, so after we graduated I asked her to marry me."

"Wow," Marie says. "That was a screw-up."

"Yup. But I'm older and wiser now," he adds, winking at Elizabeth.

"Counting on it," Elizabeth replies softly, nodding toward Marie.

Irene looks at Elizabeth and asks, "Isn't it awkward for you and Shane to live so close to her on the same island, only half-an-hour away?"

"It's a mixed bag," Elizabeth replies, rolling her eyes. "But I understand her now. I don't feel threatened and Shane doesn't indulge her theatrics. Being nearby is good for Billy because he can spend time with her and it's not a big production for us to drive him back and forth. We have our own life here, a good life surrounded by nature and wildlife and books."

"I did notice a few books in your library," Brad remarks.

"Yeah, that's how you can tell where we live. We are a family that reads."

"I remember that," Brad says. "When I saw how all three of you devoured books at the ranch, that was my first clue that you and Shane and Billy might be good for one another."

He leans forward, sets down his wine glass and turns more serious. "So explain to me, Shane, how in the world did Judy get on the inside with these white supremacists?"

"She saw this card on a bulletin board for a women's bible study group led by a macho guy, Jerry Buckley, who turns out to be the son of the local racist fossil, Buford Boh Buckley."

Robert wrinkles his brow. "Bible study? What happened to the wild Judy you were just describing? I didn't think . . ."

"I guess she thought religion was worth a try. Jerry may be a preacher's kid but he's also a major ladies man and the heir apparent to his dad's land and ministry, for lack of a better word. And he's very adept at projecting a certain image on social media. The bible part is just camouflage for the Buckleys' political and racist agendas.

"Holy crap," Marie interjects. "Pardon my language but doesn't that scare you with Billy?"

"Absolutely," Shane says. "I don't want these creeps anywhere near Billy. When I realized who she was dating I threw a fit and that's when Judy said she would be a mole for us."

"Is that a good idea?" Robert asks.

"No," Shane says. "It's terrible. I *begged* her to get out of the relationship," his voice breaking. "There's no way our department would authorize someone like Judy to go under cover but she wouldn't listen. She doesn't have the stability to manage such an intense situation. Now she says she's afraid of what Jerry will do if she tries to end it. They're involved sexually and he's used to getting his way, and now we haven't seen or heard from her in three days. She wasn't at the memorial event today."

Shane pauses for a moment. "Three days wouldn't worry me unduly but Judy says they're stockpiling guns and explosives."

"Oh boy," Robert says.

"Yeah, and the last thing she said was that she felt something big was brewing. Jerry was spending a lot of time with a couple of guys she hadn't seen before, and he'd become more distant, tense and tight-lipped."

Shane turns away and stares at a spot in the distance, suddenly far away.

*

Raised voices bring Judy to the window. Two men stand close together by the barn, face to face. An arm comes up and delivers a sharp push on the shoulder. Then, from nowhere a wicked fist smashes a nose. The victim reels back, blood spurting. His hands rush up to block the next blow, leaving his stomach undefended. A rapid left and a right to the midsection lay him face down in the dirt, wheezing, moaning, fighting for air.

Now the feet take over. Steel-toed boots find ribs and stomach, groin and kidneys, working their way up one side and down the other. The victim rolls and curls, absorbing the blows, unable to protect himself.

Judy feels sick.

The barn door swings open and Jerry emerges with both arms in the air. "That's enough, Ray! Enough," Jerry shouts. "He didn't mean anything."

"I say when it's enough," Cobb replies. With all his might, he kicks the bloody head one more time. The victim no longer moves.

Shaking, Judy watches, unable to turn away. Till she heard the men's voices, she was lying awake in the darkness waiting for Jerry, thinking about Shane and her son, Billy. Now she wraps both arms around herself and sinks to the floor in the corner, rocking back and forth.

What is going on here?

Rising unsteadily to her feet again and peering out the window, she watches Jerry run to his car and drive over to the barn. Several men lift the victim into Jerry's car, and he drives away. The bully, Ray somebody, turns his back and disappears back into the barn.

Oh god, she's alone in this compound now. This is what these people do to their friends! Jerry is gone and she's stuck here with this man who just beat one of his own people to a bloody pulp.

Hours later the sound of an approaching car pulls her away from her thoughts. The car stops in the loose pea gravel out front and she hears one door open and then close, followed seconds later by the jingle of keys in the cabin door lock. She's shaking again, hoping it's Jerry – alone – and not the guy with the steel-toed boots and eyes full of hate.

She lies frozen without turning and watches the door swing open. In the shadows she makes out a familiar profile.

"Jerry?" She asks.

"It's me."

He enters and relocks the door from the inside, then does something with the keys she doesn't see.

A wave of relief comes over her but she knows she must stay on his good side. "Come here, you big lug. Where have you been? I've missed you."

"It's ok. I'm back now. Had to take a guy to the hospital."

Judy knows better than to ask.

"Come and hold me." She throws back the covers as Jerry lays something heavy on the table – a gun? – pulls off his boots and unbuckles his belt. He steps out of his jeans with one leg, then the other, and folds his pants over the back of a chair.

Within seconds he's in the bed with her, and soon the headboard is thumping against the wall.

"Yes! Yes!" Judy screams. Her heart isn't in it, but it's the only way she knows to protect herself.

*

"You said this mole business is not an official county sheriff's investigation?" Robert asks.

"No, it's an off-the-books thing Judy fell into," Shane replies. "So I'm out on a limb with my boss."

Marie rolls her eyes.

Her gesture needs no translation. "Yeah, my thoughts exactly." Shane shakes his head and casts his eyes at the floor. "I'm growing more worried by the hour. We've got an unsanctioned, freelance mole who's my ex-wife and the mother of my son, and a total loose cannon. It'll be a miracle if she doesn't blow it."

Brad looks up. "Given everything that's on your mind right now, can you really afford to be on vacation with us?"

"Absolutely," Shane says. "First, I don't even know for sure if there's a problem. Judy may be just fine. Second, my department is on top of the whole situation. So whether I work the next couple of weeks or not, others are working."

Brad is not convinced.

"Obviously," Shane continues, "I have a personal interest and I'm keeping an eye on things, but this is our time together and I'm not about to lose it. I've been looking forward to it for months."

Marie gets up, walks behind Shane's chair and puts her hand on his shoulder. "Does this Jerry know about you and Billy?" she asks.

"Judy insists he doesn't, but if Jerry or his dad suspect she isn't on the level, or they find out about the connection to me, there's no telling what they could get out of her. I'm worried they'll torture her for information, maybe even kill her."

Irene looks worried. "Where did you say Billy is right now again?"

"Down the road at the neighbors' place," Elizabeth replies.

"In light of what we've just heard, should we go get him and keep him a little closer till this gets cleared up?" Irene asks.

"That's a good idea."

Elizabeth puts down her glass. "He'll be excited to see you anyway."

The two women head down the driveway. Elizabeth waits till they're part way down the road, then confides to Irene, "This is worse than I thought. I didn't realize Judy was missing. I haven't seen Shane like this before. Apparently he's been holding a lot in."

"He's hurting," Irene agrees. "He's tough but I think he needs support right now from all of us."

"I'm wondering how much we should tell Billy."

"Not too much just yet," Irene replies. "Let's not worry him. Besides, we've got something in the car that is going to put a big smile on his face."

*

"What is it?" Billy asks when Irene tells him there's something in the car he needs to open.

"I don't know," Irene says. "The suspense is killing us. It's heavy and it's from Bolivar, and it has your name on it. He wouldn't give us any clues."

Billy's eyes widen. "Can we go and open it right now?"

"Absolutely," Elizabeth says, peering over the top rim of her glasses like a librarian. "You've got to solve this mystery for us."

Irene smiles at the memory of last summer. The minute Billy and his dad, Shane, arrived at the Haraldsen ranch in Idaho, Billy bonded with the Basque foreman, Bolivar. They were inseparable – fishing, hiking and riding horses together. For a city kid it was the vacation of a lifetime. In fact, that was the moment the city kid turned into a country kid, and look at him now! Bolivar taught Billy to play the harmonica. Now, it seems, the Bolivar magic is back.

It makes her smile to see it. A year makes a big difference in a young boy's life and Billy is growing up, but he hasn't forgotten his Idaho adventure. Kids change so fast in the early years. He's a tall, string bean now like his dad, with a mop of brown hair, and Irene can already see the resemblance to Shane – handsome, studious and confident. But he still has the same boyish enthusiasm she saw in Idaho.

Together, the two women and Billy hike the quarter mile back to the inn at double time. Moose runs ahead and Billy goes straight to the car. Brad, Shane, Martin and Marie come out on the deck to watch.

"It's a box," Billy declares. "A heavy one!"

"Open it," Robert urges.

Billy tears at the paper. "I need scissors," he yells. "There's duct tape all over it."

"I'm pretty sure Bolivar did that to slow you down," Brad laughs. "As if anything could slow you."

Shane retreats into the house and emerges a moment later with scissors, which he hands to Billy. Finally, Billy gets a flap free, claws at the top, and then reaches inside.

"Rocks!" he yells, then buries his head again as he digs deeper, emerging with a handful of plastic baggies, all carefully labeled.

"This one's an opal," he says, "and there's pumice, and sandstone, and jade, and obsidian. Oh wow, here's silver ore!" He rummages deeper and comes up with a small bag. "And this is a gold nugget! With a note."

He unfolds the note and starts to read: "I got this from the

Yankee Fork River. It's the biggest nugget I've ever found and I thought of you. Next time you come to Idaho, let's go gold panning together."

Billy looks up at the group with a huge grin. "This is cool!"

"Here," Irene says, handing Billy her cell phone. "Give Bolivar a call. It'll make his day to hear from you."

*

Judy lies atop the bed, sweating, in thong panties and a brassiere. The afternoon is hot and this Victoria's Secret show is not entirely for purposes of seduction; it's the only underwear she has in this cabin. She was wearing it under her blouse and jeans the night Jerry took her captive. That was a shock! She was dressed for a one-nighter and suddenly found she was unable to leave.

Now, with no change of clothes for three days, it's this or nothing at all. From time to time she washes her delicates in the sink and hangs them on a coat peg to dry.

This is bad and getting worse. She's totally at the mercy of men who are increasingly intense and erratic, and that includes Jerry. Eyes closed, she listens for the telltale scuff of boots on the gravel. The guard peeks through the window every hour or two, but today he's more attentive. She's sure the men in the barracks talk about her.

She doesn't know if this peep show is a good or bad idea, but hopes it buys her some goodwill with the guards. With this group she senses it's best to go all in – give them something to stay on their good side. She knows she doesn't fit the typical female profile in this compound where the women are hard. She's the exact opposite, soft and sexy.

Everyone knows she's Jerry's property; she doubts any of the foot soldiers will make a move against her. But the men Jerry has been spending time with seem capable of anything.

She'd like to know what Jerry does with them in the evenings, and why. He won't say but usually returns after midnight.

Till he returns she's alone with her thoughts and the eyes that peek through the tiny window every hour or so, scanning the room for a brief moment. They find her on the bed like this, where she pretends to doze. Then they go away and the retreating boots scuff some more on the gravel till she can hear them no longer.

She didn't see this coming; captivity was a total surprise. One night she and Jerry made love. The next morning he got up and dressed in his khaki uniform and beret, and locked the door as he left, "for your own safety," he said. The lock is a double cylinder; she can't unlock it from the inside and the windows are barred and too small. She assumes the little cabin was designed partly with confinement in mind. But why is she here?

*

In the rural town of Snohomish, north of Seattle, a middle-aged man in blue jeans and a denim shirt counts out a dozen, well-circulated $100 bills and lays them on the counter in front of a pig-tailed clerk in a checkered shirt. She carries pruning shears in a holster on her belt.

"That is some serious storage," she says with a smile. "Making some upgrades to your manure system?"

The man stares at her without response, his expression inscrutable and unchanging.

She drops the attempt at small talk, scoops up the bills, rubs her fingers on a couple of them, holds them up to the light, checks the serial numbers on the newer ones, and then rings up the transaction. She tucks the $100 bills under the drawer in her till and hands the man $23.47 in change and two copies of his receipt.

"You're taking this with you today?" the clerk asks. "What are you driving?"

"The Budget rental truck out front."

"Pull around back and give the yellow copy to the young man in the yard," she instructs, "and he'll load it for you."

The man steps outside, pulls a Lucky Strike from behind his ear and lights it. He takes several puffs. Then he climbs into the cab of the truck and drives back to the yard. It's raining lightly, unusual but not unheard of for Puget Sound in the summertime.

Moments later, with much loud beeping, a yellow forklift reaches into a stack of shrink-wrapped pallets, inserts its forks into the one on the top and lifts it free of the stack. The young operator backs up the forklift, turns it smartly, and carries the load across the yard to the waiting truck, where he lines up with the open cargo bay and deposits the pallet carefully on the deck. The forklift driver then backs up, realigns the forks and gives the pallet a push forward with his machine.

When he has done as much as he can with the machine, he hops down from his seat and pushes the pallet the last few feet into the truck.

The truck driver acknowledges him wordlessly with a touch of his brim, rolls down the cargo door, jumps into the diver's seat and pulls away from the farm store.

Ten minutes later, the Budget truck climbs a freeway access ramp and merges into the heavy stream of afternoon traffic northbound toward Everett on Interstate 405.

*

Judy stares at a patch of sunshine through the tiny sliding window. Jerry showed up at two a.m. and left again at ten, locking the door behind him. The day is especially bright and fresh after a rare summer rain overnight. The dim cabin, Judy's cell, is lit only by a single desk lamp. The one-room cabin reminds her of the tiny, low-cost housing she's read about for homeless people.

The cabin is adequate but she's bored, frustrated, cut off and scared. A toilet and sink occupy one corner, behind a partition. She has no radio or TV. Except for the bars, she supposes this is typical of much of the housing at the compound for single men who make up the security detail.

Through the window, Judy watches a heavyset old woman in a tent-style dress leave the farmhouse and waddle across the compound toward her. The woman sways from side to side, her whole torso rocking, breathing with effort, carrying a plate of what Judy suspects is more tuna noodle casserole and fruit. The matronly woman approaches the cabin and knocks at the sliding window. Judy opens it.

"Here you go, dear, some lunch," the lady announces in a kindly voice as she slides the plate through the opening. "How are you getting along?"

"I'm going crazy," Judy replies. "I need exercise. I need something to read," she says, gesturing toward the desk.

"You really should read the bible," the old lady advises, still catching her breath. "It will explain everything. Study the word and you'll understand these turbulent times."

"Do you understand them?" Judy asks.

35

Ida Mae does not answer.

"This isn't right, you know," Judy says. "None of it. If Jerry loved me he'd never treat me this way."

"He loves you," the woman assures her.

Judy's not sure anymore.

Jerry's mom, Ida Mae, is an exception to the tattooed look of most in this compound. Judy sizes her up as a traditional Midwestern farm wife of her generation. Is she senile? She's clearly on some other planet, but if there's any hope at all of getting someone in this compound to help her, Judy thinks Ida Mae is it.

"This is all for your own well being," Ida Mae says, "even though you may not understand it. It's not our place as women to question. Jerry asked me to keep you comfortable and that's what I'm doing."

"Well I'm not comfortable in the least!"

"Everything will make sense in time if you trust in the Lord. The answers are in the Book of Revelations."

"Revelations!" Judy screams. "Seriously? You tell Jerry in this country, people don't just lock up other people and get away with it."

"Pray to the lord for patience and understanding. I know this is hard but it'll soon all make sense."

"This is crazy," Judy insists.

The old lady frowns. "These are the end times. Jesus is coming. The unclean races are making their last stand, and God's white legions are rising up. My husband, Buford Boh, has been warning about this all his life. The white race are God's people, but so many today have lost sight of that."

This old woman is crazy as a cuckoo. And she's obsessed with tuna! This stuff is puke! But that's the least of Judy's problems. Something very sinister is going on in this compound. She's got to get out and alert Shane. But how?

*

The box truck from Snohomish sits by a freshly tilled farm field on a country roadside on Fir Island, in the Skagit River Delta. The orange-white-and-blue "Budget" logo, which had been prominent on the truck's sides and back, now reads "Economy" in green-and-white.

The large, static-cling decals cover all the identifying areas nicely.

In the cab, the lone occupant, Ray Cobb, reclines across the seat with a red-and-white Make America Great cap pulled low across his forehead, shading his eyes from the afternoon sun. A sweet breeze, mixed with the vague aroma of ripe steer manure, wafts through the cab.

Cobb has been napping but is stirring now. Under the bill of his cap, he looks across the black earth of the river bottom and studies a panoramic, picture-postcard view of Mount Baker and all its snowy flanks, nearest of the volcanoes in the Cascade Range.

He opens the glove box and rummages through the contents till he finds his cigarettes. He pulls one from the pack, inserts it between his lips and digs his lighter from his front pocket. He flicks it several times until he gets a flame. As his cigarette starts to burn, he clicks the lighter shut. Several breaths later, he feels his nerves settle down.

He studies the pastoral view. This is a far cry from Arkansas, he thinks.

After leaving Snohomish, Cobb chooses this back road to route himself off the interstate and away from weigh stations and ferry crossings where he might attract too much curiosity from state police. Traffic past the truck this afternoon on this sleepy back road has been steady but light. He hasn't seen any police or state patrol all day.

He starts the engine and shifts into gear, following the country road west and north across the flat landscape. He passes a crew of farm laborers working in a field, hoeing and bending over plants. Those damn beaners. He wonders how many of them are in the country illegally. A long plume of dust rises into the air behind a large tractor pulling a set of discs. Before long he comes to a sandwich board for "immodest" ice cream cones. He makes an impulsive decision and pulls over to the shoulder across from a large farm produce stand.

He shuts off the engine and gets out, then crosses the road and makes his way past clusters of tourists and tables of produce to the cashier's table. There, he orders an obscenely large, hand-dipped, chocolate waffle cone.

Refreshed by two big mouthfuls of ice cream off the top of the cone, he wanders among tables piled high with apples, blueberries, potatoes, broccoli, cabbage, asparagus and corn. Finally he returns to the cab with the rest of his treat, catching drips of melting ice cream in a wad of flimsy napkins. This is making a mess.

One-handed now, he starts the engine and shifts into gear. The truck labors up a small rise to a bridge over the North Fork of the Skagit River and continues along Pleasant Ridge. This backcountry route to the Anacortes area and Deception Pass keeps him away from heavily-traveled freeways, where state police concentrate their patrols.

As he leaves Fir Island behind he enters a stretch of mostly wooded country for a few miles. In time the trees give way to elegant, century-old farmhouses looking out at a patchwork of fields and crops spread across the broad Skagit River valley. The farms here seem large and prosperous. The road follows the ridge, then descends onto the flats, where he comes to an intersection. He turns left, following the signs toward LaConner, past dairy and tulip fields.

Within a few minutes he arrives on the outskirts of a picturesque waterfront village on the banks of a saltwater channel. Signs point to Carla's Cupboard and Vintage Antiques, Bayside Books and the Artist's Loft. They reflect an affluent lifestyle he cannot imagine. This is obviously a tourist town, so he bypasses the congested downtown area and stays with the two-lane highway up an incline and across an orange, arching bridge over Swinomish Channel onto an Indian reservation.

Suddenly he's surrounded by dilapidated houses, fishnets, cars sitting up on blocks, dogs, bicycles and backyard boats lining the reservation's main street. Here and there, someone sits on a porch. A sign on one house reads, "Palm Reader" and another says "Shaker Church." Ahead is a complex of tribal buildings – the community hall and health center. His heart pounds. Disgust and rage well up in him. Looking at all this, he can see what's wrong with America right in front of him.

On the far side of the channel, the view is of prosperity and civilization. But on this side it's just poverty and government handouts, shiftless people with no ambition.

His stomach tightens. This is exactly what weighs down the social welfare system and drains the livelihood of working Americans. These people wallow in alcoholism and disease, live off the income from gambling casinos and churn out babies who will never contribute anything to society. They are the rot that ruins America for the white race. He wants no part of this scum.

Chapter 7

Brad and his companions look out across the huge crowd in the parking lot of the town's large shopping center. Dozens of signs and banners declare their sentiments: *No Homeland for Bigots, Impeach* and *Decency is Greatness.* Others state simply *Make America Good* and *Make America Kind.*

Sheriff's deputies, some in police cruisers and others on foot, watch over the orderly group. The officers all wear walkie-talkies strapped to their chests.

The group from the inn have risen early for this and walked the mile to town. Shane is wearing cutoffs and a sport shirt, and some leather sandals. Deputies directing traffic at intersections wave at him and taunt him gently with wolf whistles. "Nice legs!"

"In your dreams," he replies.

Shane predicts this will be the largest public demonstration and march ever held on the island – the community's response to the supremacist rally held at the state park. After leaving the inn at 10 a.m., they joined families, couples and individuals already walking toward the town's large shopping mall.

The scene is inspiring but Brad never expected people would have to take to the streets to defend decency and civility.

"It came together on social media," Shane says. "It was just an idea a few days ago. Many in the community are shaken by what they see happening and the tone coming from the White House. Word spread like wildfire. They got a parade permit, so it's all legit. But I'm sure Fox News will call us hooligans."

"Are we looking at the beginnings of a civil uprising?" Marie asks.

"I don't know; I think it's possible," Elizabeth replies. "The

40

two sides don't agree on anything. Nothing like this has ever happened on the island. That guy with the white hair is a retired NASA scientist. The woman with the sign is director of the homeless coalition. I recognize several teachers, retired professors, Iraq veterans, some high school students – a cross section of the community."

Brad estimates the crowd at several thousand, remarkable for such a small community.

A sheriff's SUV with flashing red and blue lights pulls into the street in front of the mall and sounds a *whoop, whoop*. Traffic stops and an officer steps into the intersection with orange cones to close the street. The sheriff's SUV pulls away at a crawl, leading a procession of demonstrators on foot.

By the time this entire crowd funnels out of the parking lot, Brad thinks the march could stretch for a mile. Alongside Shane and Elizabeth, he falls into step and they work their way up Main Street, then left onto East Harbor Avenue toward the bay. Up ahead, he watches the front of the procession turn left and head for Freeland Park, where tents, canopies and banners flutter in the breeze.

When they arrive at the shoreline park, the aroma of hot dogs and mustard fills the air. Speakers from local churches and civic groups are just getting started.

"It raises my spirits to see such a huge turnout," Robert remarks. "It restores my faith that the vast majority of people are decent and caring."

"It really does. But I can't stop worrying about Judy. I'd feel a whole lot better if I knew she was okay," Shane says.

"What about paying a visit to Jerry Buckley?" Brad asks. "He and Judy were dating so doesn't it make sense to approach him and ask some questions?"

"Under normal circumstances I'd say yes. But in this case, if we approach Jerry with questions it could make him wonder about her, and put her in greater danger. Assuming Judy's cover is still good, I think it's better if we don't tip our hand to Jerry that we're looking for her."

Shane explains that Jerry lives at his dad's compound in the woods near Lagoon Point. Several households of the extended family live there behind a gate and a watchtower. It's a paramilitary reserve with a barracks for what they call their soldiers.

"Even if we went there and asked for Jerry, we wouldn't get past the gate without a search warrant," Shane says. "No judge is going to authorize a warrant without some reasonable grounds for suspicion."

"Then," Brad says, "we'll have to find a more creative way."

*

In the parlor of the Eagles Inn, Elizabeth peers through stylish reading glasses at her laptop. Glasses are her indulgence – that and books. Shane is always laughing about the glasses and these are especially distinctive with a pebble design on the temples, like rocks on the beach. She sips her coffee as she scrolls through the weekly newspaper online. An article about the local sanctuary city campaign catches her eye and she studies it for several minutes.

She turns to Marie. "Can you believe this reader comment? Sanctuary Group Opens Door to Islamic Law in Langley."

"Islamic Law?" Marie leans down to read the screen. "you mean amputations and stoning? Is that an imminent problem here?" she asks, laughing.

"Apparently in the minds of some," Elizabeth says. "This new administration is stirring up all kinds of fears. Some people have the idea that if we open the door a crack by declaring Langley a sanctuary city, thousands of Muslims will move to the island and ruin the community."

She continues, "But what I really wanted to say was this – look who wrote the comment."

"Camille Norlie," Marie says. "Who's that?"

"No one!" Elizabeth replies. "That's just it. There's no such person. Those of us on the committee have been trying for months to find out who she is. She has a minimal Facebook page with no picture and only three friends, and claims to be a graduate of our high school, but we've talked with people in every class going back decades and no one ever heard of her."

"I knew there were reports of fake accounts and meddling with public opinion at the national level," Marie says, "but I never imagined it happening at the community level. Does anyone know this woman's Facebook friends? Has anyone talked to them? Do they vouch for her?"

"They don't know her personally, either – just friended her because they like her views. It's pretty obviously a fake identity. We've identified a couple of other nonexistent people, too, who are posting comments to newspaper articles and weighing-in on Facebook on the sanctuary conversation."

"So who's behind this?"

"We think it's someone connected to local government. In fact we think we know who it is, based on the syntax and phrasing, but don't want to say without proof."

"Wow," Irene remarks. "Political intrigue in the little village by the sea. It's shades of the Unabomber case where they identified the suspect from the way he put words together in the manifesto he sent to the newspapers. What a shame that we've come to this in local politics – neighbors hiding behind fake identities to influence other neighbors."

*

Elizabeth pulls the plastic wrap off a couscous salad and places it on the long table at the front of the church social hall, alongside plates of pita, hummus, tahini, falafel, baklava, lamb kebabs and other Middle Eastern dishes she cannot name. Conversation fills the room as friends, mostly standing and circulating through the crowd, catch up with one another.

"This is a quite a spread," Marie remarks. "I wouldn't have imagined an interfaith potluck with Muslims in a sleepy village like Langley."

"Isn't it something?" Elizabeth replies. "It reflects what I consider the real character of the community, which is progressive, welcoming and inclusive."

"I have to say that inviting Muslim guests to a potluck at a Christian church is the exact opposite of the nationalist hate rally at the park the other day, which was also dressed up as Christianity," Marie remarks.

"Quite a contrast, isn't it? The local community does this several times a year."

Irene watches a silver-haired man take the podium and switch on his microphone, then tap it several times it till the room falls silent.

"The van from Seattle will arrive in just a few minutes," he announces. "After we welcome our guests, let's invite them to go through the line first and fill their plates with food, and then the rest of us will do the same. After we eat, we'll ask them to give us a short program and talk about their experiences."

Through windows on the side of the recreation hall Irene watches a van pull into the alley behind the church. Doors swing open and several olive-skinned children emerge, talking excitedly in a language Irene does not recognize, followed by parents and grandparents, some with stooped backs, walking with the support of canes. This is something she's never seen in Stanley, Idaho. The women wear the hijab. Their driver, a dashing, dark-haired man in his thirties with a neatly trimmed beard, shows them into the reception hall.

As the master of ceremonies welcomes them in English, the driver translates into what Irene assumes must be Arabic. Then the guests proceed to the potluck table, fill their plates and disperse to tables throughout the room. Children gravitate to a play area at the side of the room where their hosts have provided coloring books and art supplies, and various games. Soon, several of the children are drawing pictures.

After lunch, the group's driver takes the microphone to introduce himself in articulate English. "Good afternoon, Langley friends. From all of us in the Muslim community of Seattle, thank you for your warm welcome and fellowship today. My name is Majed and I will introduce the others who came over on the ferry with me today, and then I'll tell you a little about the group because I know you're curious."

Irene is listening to every word, trying to remember the details so she can share them later with Brad. Majed is a software engineer who came to the United States ten years ago and now volunteers with recently-arrived immigrants to help them acclimate to life in their new country. "And let me just say, we are all here legally!" he adds, drawing a laugh and a round of applause from the Langley crowd.

"Imagine," Majed says, "you are seventy years old and you have some health problems, and the apartment building you own is bombed to rubble. It is your whole retirement – the work of a lifetime – and now it is gone, and you have nothing."

This, he says, is the story of Mr. Abati, pointing toward one of the gentlemen in the group. After years of waiting, Mr. Abati was finally approved to emigrate to the United States and join other family members here. But he has nothing left now and is starting over in a strange new culture.

"I can't imagine it," Irene says. "If that happened to Brad and me at this age, I don't know what we'd do."

The driver introduces Hiya, a little girl, age nine, to sing about her hometown of Aleppo, Syria. It's a beautiful, old city with thousands of years of culture, he says.

In blue jeans and a print shirt, Hiya could pass for any American kid of her age, though Irene notices she doesn't smile. The girl takes the wireless microphone as if she'd done it before and begins to sing with surprising confidence and poise. But about a minute into the song her voice breaks. She sings a little more, then can't continue. She puts down the microphone, turns away and begins to cry. The driver rushes to give her a hug and lead her to a chair. The audience applauds.

Majed explains in English that the beautiful city of Aleppo is just rubble now, and that Hiya's brother and best friend died in the fighting.

Irene feels a tear roll down her own cheek. She reaches up and brushes it away. "This breaks my heart. No child should have to go through that – any part of it."

"When you meet these people in person, it really hits home," Elizabeth agrees. "You can't listen to their stories without feeling we have to do something. I want to believe most Americans are compassionate people who want to help."

She explains that the church has been reaching out to the Seattle Muslim community for a couple of years to bring a few of the recent immigrants here for an afternoon. "It's just to give them a few hours in a normal place where they aren't treated as vermin and terrorists but are welcomed warmly by everyday Americans. Majed says these potluck receptions in Langley are a highlight of their experience in America, a rare chance to meet ordinary Americans."

Chapter 8

The irony of vacations to Brad is that the change of routine is both relaxing and exhausting. People can't wait to go on vacation, but once they get there, then they can't wait to get home.

He finds it hard to keep his eyes open in the evenings when the others sit round the dinner table or in the parlor and talk. Tonight he excuses himself early and retires to the bedroom.

Moments after lying down on the bed, he finds himself drifting. Soon he's in a motel swimming pool. His first love, Bella, swims toward him as he hoists himself up on the pool's edge in a big flood of water. It drains from his head and swim trunks. She laughs and reaches for a hand up. He hoists her up beside him in a sopping wet pool of her own. She is all black hair and water and flesh.

They have it to themselves – this pool, this sultry night in the nearly vacant auto court, far from anyone who knows them. Bella's hair sticks to her back; she doesn't even have a bathing cap. She gives herself to him in this moment with a look Brad has never seen before. They sit there dripping, watching the sky darken with towering, black clouds. The rumble of thunder rolls through the Tennessee hills.

"This is crazy," Brad says. "We going to get killed out here," and they grab their towels and race back to the room.

Inside, they flip the deadbolt behind them, peel off their suits in the shower and collapse onto the bed. They don't even discuss it. They are registered as "Mr. and Mrs. Brad Haraldsen" but they are not married. This is their first time. Their bodies are wet and steamy and Bella is beautiful beyond Brad's wildest dreams. He bends toward her lips, feels her hips against his. This is really happening.

*

Brad jolts awake with a start, his heart pounding. He's back in the Eagles Inn, shivering, cold and wet. His T-shirt and pillow are soaked. It has happened again, for the third time on this trip. He slides his legs out of bed slowly in the darkened room, not to awaken Irene. Teeth chattering on this warm summer evening, he feels in his suitcase for a dry T-shirt, finds one and opens the door with a barely perceptible click.

Across the hall in the bathroom he pulls two plush towels from the stack, returns to the bedroom and folds back the covers on his side, laying down one towel on the bottom sheet and the other on the pillow. He pulls the covers over himself and shakes till the warmth returns.

He feels guilty about the dream but also deeply, profoundly happy. It seems a betrayal somehow of his wife, yet he has never stopped wanting Bella more than anyone in the world. With her death several years ago at Deception Pass Bridge, that door closed forever. Yet yet, for one moment in his dreams, she is right here in this bed with him, as real as can be.

He wonders if Bella's spirit ever left this island, or whether instead she lives here for eternity now, just out of sight in a dimension only he can visit. Does Shane have these dreams as well? Or does Bella come only to Brad in the night because it was he she always loved, with the burning love that always eluded them?

She is a mystery now, in death as she was in life. Her power over him, over men, was undeniable. Are her visits telling him she ached for him, for what they had for one night in Gatlinburg, Tennessee? Or are they just the random, screwy workings of an old man's brain, chemicals and neurons sloshing around in his pleasure center, giving him one last self-serving fantasy of his own delusional making?

Privately he wonders if it's something worse. Is this the first telltale sign of the last great mental decline everyone dreads in later life?

He cannot breathe a word of this to Irene. Those who say spouses have no secrets don't live in the real world. This must remain his secret alone. As for the other secret, the one he and Irene discussed, she will keep that one, he believes, though she struggles with it. She challenged him on it the minute he asked her to say nothing.

"Don't you think our friends are entitled to know?" Irene asked.

"Yes, but not now," Brad said. "It will change the whole visit."

What Brad wants for these two weeks is to rekindle in Shane and Elizabeth's new home the chemistry and camaraderie that happened with this group a year ago at his ranch in Stanley. That visit was the high point of his life.

"We are here for Shane and Elizabeth and Billy," he tells Irene. "There will be more than enough time for the other, some other time."

But how long can he hide what's happening from them?

*

The aroma of fir and cedar hangs in the warm afternoon atmosphere as Brad, Irene and Shane climb through a meadow of sword ferns. Tall trees shade the forest path, but spears of sunlight pierce the canopy and light up patches of ferns.

Somewhere close, a Great-horned Owl calls in that distinctive, muffled voice that seems to come from anywhere and everywhere. Brad scans the big firs about thirty feet up, checking the dead stubs of branches near the trunk till he spots the familiar dark profile with its two pointed ear-tufts. Those tufts make it look fierce, Brad thinks, but its real ferocity is its silent stealth and razor-sharp claws. Owls make no sound when they swoop down on their prey.

"Slow down for a minute, will you please?" Irene asks.

Brad wonders if she's slowing the pace for him.

"I can't sketch as fast as you two walk." Brad is secretly relieved because he's short of breath. Irene studies a sword fern growing out of a decomposing log, scratching with a pen at a small artist's pad in her hand.

Brad cocks his head.

Pock . . . pock . . . pock.

"Hairy Woodpecker," Shane remarks.

"You're reading my mind," Brad replies. He can see that the old snags and nurse logs are perfect for them. The trees in this mature forest are so big that when they fall they decompose over decades and even hundreds of years. The wood fills up with bugs and provides nutrients for new trees to grow right out of the fallen ones.

"We always see or hear a few woodpeckers when we walk the Wilbert Trail," Shane says.

"How close are we to the Buckley compound?"

"Maybe a mile as the crow flies."

"Spoken like a birder," Brad laughs.

"We're also only a mile or two from the safe house where that neo-Nazi bank robber fought it out with the feds 30 years ago, and just a few miles from several other safe houses that members of his gang used here on Whidbey."

"It helps to see this place," Brad says, "helps me get a sense of where some of these events happened."

"The rally Martin and I attended the other day was just across the highway in the park's main campground area. That's the busier part of this park. "When I go for a walk, I prefer to do it over here on the Wilbert Trail."

"The trees are beyond anything we have in Idaho," Brad says.

"Look up at the canopy," Shane suggests. "It's easy to forget we're in a three-dimensional space."

Brad leans way back and cranes his neck. His head swims and he staggers sideways before regaining his balance. He's a bit light headed.

"Ok," Irene says, watching him. "We're staying right here for a few minutes." She scratches at the pad again. Brad finds a log and sits down.

He can see that while they've been talking, the trail entered a very different ecosystem from the one where they started. They are in a wetland now, surrounded by water. Parts of the trail are on a boardwalk. Not only that, but the water is pristine – ultra clear. Sunlight penetrates to the bottom in places where it pierces through the canopy. The air here is cool and refreshing.

The sword ferns they saw earlier have given way to delicate deer ferns, which he knows thrive in wet, shady habitats. By the trailside he sees the yellow flower of the skunk cabbage. The trees in this spot are mostly cedars, which favor moist settings. Anyone stepping off the trail would have some very difficult hiking.

"These really aren't old growth in the strict sense," Shane says, pointing out the trees. "But many of them go back hundreds of years and were passed over when foresters first logged the island because they were misshapen or too hard to get to. So these trees have been left alone for a long, long time."

Brad is still thinking about The Ancient Cedar, one of the signature trees they passed earlier on this trail. It's about five hundred years old, dating back to the time of Columbus. He has long felt that trees place our human lifespans in perspective. The Ancient Cedar was growing here unnoticed and undisturbed while the American Revolution, the Civil War and all the subsequent world wars and social movements took place.

He recalls that Shane said South Whidbey State Park is one of the few good examples on the island of a mixed-species forest of many age classes growing side by side. This is what a real forest is like, it strikes him, not a monoculture of one species, started all at the same time by someone replanting a logged forest. It crosses his mind that the supremacists want a monoculture of sorts, too.

"What's it like at the Buckley compound?" Brad asks. "Is it this same kind of thing – a tree canopy like this? Can you tell much from studying aerial photography or Google Earth?"

"You can see a lot," Shane explains – "the general layout of houses and buildings. But there's also a lot you can't see. They've got guards and cameras, and don't allow any outsiders past the gate. We don't have a complete picture of what's there. We think they've put some of it underground."

"I'm trying to imagine how something like that can exist in the twenty-first century, only miles from the office towers of the Puget Sound metropolitan core."

"It's by no means unheard of. You'd be surprised at how many of these gated, survivalist-type compounds and private estates there are on this island and others around Puget Sound. Some are owned by wealthy executives in the tech or entertainment industries. They see things breaking down in the social order and want a secure getaway or safe house where they can ride out trouble if it happens."

"Seriously?" Brad asks.

"Absolutely. This has been going on quietly for years."

"What are they preparing for?"

"Pretty much any natural or man-made disaster, anything from a volcanic eruption to an electromagnetic pulse attack, an outbreak of Ebola, worldwide economic collapse, regional mega-quake or anything else that might cause widespread disease or famine. They're equipping themselves with everything from hand-crank radios to home smelters to melt lead for bullets."

"And this really is taking hold?"

"It's spreading, thanks to the Internet. There's a whole online network to bring together survivalists with the suppliers who sell what they need to equip their properties."

"I had no idea," Brad remarks. "Was there any link between the people at the Buckley compound and the guys who got into the shootout here with the FBI?"

"We never found any," Shane says. "But these people know who their friends and sympathizers are all over the country. Philosophically, I'm sure they knew the Buckley compound was nearby, a safe haven of sorts. They took comfort in being close to the preacher Buckley and the kindred spirits who get their ideas from him."

*

Elizabeth runs a vacuum cleaner over the Oriental rug in the lodge's dining room while Marie and Robert load tablecloths and dishtowels into the washing machine. "Thanks for helping out," Elizabeth tells them when she shuts off the noisy vacuum. "I had a feeling this day was coming."

Maria, her housekeeper, had always been punctual, Elizabeth says, but today she didn't appear. She had mentioned a few weeks ago that she might have to go away suddenly, and if so, she was sorry. She wasn't sure yet.

"One by one, maids, caregivers, housekeepers, gardeners, carpenters and laborers have quietly disappeared from businesses all over the island," Elizabeth says. "Latinos who have lived and worked on the island for years suddenly fear they'll be arrested at any moment and shipped back to Mexico or Central America. They are selling what little they had and leaving – self-deporting."

"It's tearing families apart," she says. "Some in the Latino community are afraid to report crime or even pick up their children from school for fear the police are watching and will hand them over to immigration officers who will deport them."

"That just isn't right," Marie observes. "There must be a more compassionate way to clear up the immigration status of people who've lived here for years. They work hard and have so little. Why go out of your way to do that to people who have families to support and are doing the very best they can to get by?"

"Because it fires up the president's base!" Elizabeth replies. "Makes him look like a law-and-order guy." She adds that parents worry when they go off to work in the morning that they might never come home that night. With that hanging over them, some are making contingency plans with relatives or friends to care for their children in case that happens. Others are selling their businesses and deporting themselves while they still have some control over their fate.

"So much is happening beneath the surface, out of sight," Marie remarks. She knows that some of these people must have no choice but to go back to countries where they or their families were in jeopardy for their lives from gang activity, abusive relationships or political conflict.

"The scare tactics are all crafted to generate fear," Elizabeth says. "It's politically useful to whip up animosity against whole groups to polarize the partisan debate. That's why the president goes on TV and labels them as rapists, murderers or terrorists."

"You're right," Marie agrees. "It's all about the base."

Elizabeth reaches for a tray and four tall glasses. She clinks ice cubes into each glass and fills them with lemonade from a pitcher in the refrigerator. It's time for a break from their morning's work, she declares, suggesting they move out to the deck for a few minutes.

As they settle into deck chairs, Marie asks, "How is all this going over with the local community?"

"It's a mixed reaction," Elizabeth says. "Some people just want the laws enforced, with no leniency. But we've got people on our Sanctuary City committee, leading citizens, whose parents and grandparents were shipped off to death camps by the Nazis in World War II as Jewish vermin. They've seen where this fear mongering and xenophobia lead. It feeds right into the identity movement, white nationalism and neo-Nazism, and eventually to crimes against humanity."

Marie shakes her head. "My dad spent his career in the Air Force. There wasn't any doubt in his mind about whether the Nazis and their sympathizers were 'very fine people' or not."

Brad listens to the conversation. In his experience every generation has to re-learn the lessons of history. Racism against one group or another has ebbed and flowed as far back as anyone can remember, and certainly throughout the history of the United States. It's an old formula that despots all over the world have revived to consolidate their influence and power.

When he and Irene chose central Idaho as their home, they wondered what kind of community they'd found. But the Stanley area is such a magnet for travelers, it attracts many from worldwide for the same reasons as Brad and Irene. They were pleasantly surprised, but only after overcoming their early reservations, knowing the state had an image tarnished by what was happening in the northern Idaho panhandle. That area and remote parts of Montana were known as havens for white separatists and survivalists, some of whom envisioned the Northwest one day as a white homeland. Others just wanted to live apart, with minimal government interference.

What added to Brad's concerns was the high profile, Christian identity preacher whose compound in Hayden Lake attracted some unsavory followers, including the guy for whom the memorial demonstration was held at the park here on Whidbey. The preacher died of natural causes in 2004 after much controversy, and the compound is now gone. But while it was there, it was a breeding ground for radical ideology.

Elizabeth interrupts his thoughts. "It's so hard to keep all these groups and ideologies straight. They go by various names but all kind of add up to different shades of the same intolerance."

"That's true," he replies. "You've got separatists, supremacists, nationalists, the Christian identity movement, fascists, neo-Nazis and others. You could lump America First in there somewhere, too. They like to think of themselves as patriots."

He adds, "And that's ironic because the identity movement sees the federal government as the enemy. Every so often it inspires a zealot such as Timothy McVeigh, who killed 168 people when he bombed the Oklahoma City Federal Building in 1995.

"McVeigh considered the bombing partly as payback for the 1992 federal siege at Ruby Ridge, Idaho," Brad says. "That arrest cost the lives of a US marshal and the wife and son of separatist Randy Weaver. And nearly eighty people died in Waco, Texas, in 1993 in another federal siege at the Branch Davidian compound. In both cases you could make a strong argument that serious mistakes and miscalculations were made on both sides. These confrontations escalated into violence that didn't need to happen, and just made everything worse."

Elizabeth sighs. "It's all so unnecessary. And now the new administration adds to the tragedy by fanning the embers of racism. It has never been easier for people like Buford Boh Buckley and his followers to wrap themselves self-righteously in the flag and religion.

*

Jerry Buckley sits down at his desk in his broadcast studio. On the wall behind him are a poster-sized red-and-black swastika and the flag of the arrow cross. He's attired in a sharply-creased, khaki shirt with a long black necktie, black beret and a red swastika armband.

It's early morning but this is when Jerry broadcasts live for followers in time zones to the east. He is well aware of the importance of symbolism. An articulate speaker, he consciously projects the handsome, youthful face of a resurgent movement long associated with old, unsophisticated white men. His black beard signals virility in contrast to the thinning white hair of his father and other long-time leaders of the movement. They had their day, but they are not the face of the future.

He powers up his computer, types the *seig heil* password and goes to the Christian Homeland Facebook page. At the top of his news feed he clicks "live video" and then "go live."

"Good morning friends, Christian nationalist soldiers and Christian women," he begins. "Jerry Buckley here for God and country."

The nod to women is deliberate, of course, because this live Facebook chat reaches many female sympathizers, young and old, some of whom live on isolated farms in the heartland or the remote mountains of Montana and Idaho. Widows, especially, often see him as a surrogate son and write large checks in response to his broadcasts.

The invocation of Christianity broadens his reach to listeners who might initially flinch at the strident tone, and gives him the aura of respectability.

He knows what he does especially well is explain current events from a Nazi and supremacist perspective, picking and choosing from the Book of Revelations to back up his forecast for listeners of the turbulent times ahead. With sufficiently vague prophecies of wars and rumors of wars, plagues, earthquakes, false gods and false prophets, it's very hard to be wrong. His broadcast is part news program, part church service and part Nazi propaganda. Much of it follows point-for-point the scenario for revolution outlined in the William Luther Pierce's novel, *The Turner Diaries*.

"These are exciting times for us," Jerry says. "After our very successful march in Charlottesville, we feel the momentum growing. This bold, straight-talking new administration in Washington, D.C., is telling the truth at last and giving our movement the recognition it deserves."

"I can't tell you everything we're doing here at Buckley headquarters. We don't telegraph our next move. But trust me, very big things are in motion behind the scenes."

This line is an understatement, of course. The terrorist plot he's sponsoring with Midwestern associates will put this whole state on the map, along with other battlegrounds that have emerged since the 1980s in Oklahoma, Texas and Idaho. But he knows he's walking a fine line, facilitating something that absolutely, positively must not be traced back to the family compound if his work is to continue.

"We just celebrated a very successful memorial for our friend and colleague who was murdered by federal agents. And here at Buckley headquarters we're preparing for the final battle to reclaim our homeland for God's people, our Sacred White Race . . ."

As heir to his dad's life's work, Jerry has taken the family business from the horse-and-buggy era to the information age.

"If you believe in our work, I hope you'll partner with us. We need your financial support to buy arms and medical supplies for the decisive battle we all know is soon to be upon us."

One by one, Facebook followers across the country check in and post comments under Jerry's live picture as he talks. One by one, credit card contributions flow to the group's PayPal account.

*

A few miles away, Shane pulls to a stop in a deserted parking area where the road ends and Puget Sound begins. He and Brad open their doors and walk to the rear of the Chevy Suburban. Shane raises the lift door and Moose jumps out. Shane clips a retractable leash to Moose's harness.

"Ready?" he asks Brad.

"Ready. We don't get many beach walks in Stanley."

"This is my favorite time of the morning," Shane explains, "when the summer sun is just coming up. The early-morning air is cool and fresh, and we'll have the whole beach to ourselves till the sun climbs over the horizon. I remember you like early mornings, too."

"You've been talking to Elizabeth," Brad replies. "We had a thing going at the ranch last summer, getting up before daybreak and sneaking off to town to do our talking while the rest of you slept. I love an early start."

"Yes, but I'm on to you now. Also, I haven't forgotten having coffee with you in the middle of the night on the Alaska Ferry."

"There was that, too. Another of our legendary early starts."

The two men head down the beach, paralleling the line of drift logs and woody debris, with Moose in the lead. He's zigzagging, sniffing and peeing, looking over his shoulder every so often to keep a watchful eye on his master.

At this hour, the Cascade Mountains behind them are backlit. There's just enough visibility to see the expanse of sand and the Olympics across the water. "The beach here is immense," Brad remarks.

"It's these summer low tides. But yeah, that's why the locals love it so much. You get these vast sand flats. This beach is a bit of a local secret, too. This is a county park, so it doesn't get the crush of tourists the state parks do. And it has an off-leash section, which the dog owners love."

Brad wonders aloud why they call it Useless Bay.

"It just isn't any good for ships," Shane says. "Early explorers couldn't bring their ships close to shore because it's too shallow. If a ship were to come in on the high tide, it would be lying on its side a few hours later."

Brad notices a sunlit, snowcapped peak to the south and recognizes the familiar profile of Mount Rainier. In the foreground, low on the horizon, he can also make out the skyline of downtown

Seattle and its tallest buildings.

They trudge along for some distance before Brad breaks the silence.

"Tell me about this Rev. Buford Boh Buckley."

"He's lived on the island forever," Shane says, "mostly out of sight and out of mind. His father homesteaded forty acres of prime forest in the Lagoon Point area when the first white settlers reached the island. They scratched out a small farm but farming never was very prosperous on a small scale. In any case the family goes way back and has some influential connections. He's a conspiracy theorist and never had much sway in the community, never really came to anyone's attention till recently. I always thought of him as all talk and no action."

"Right."

"He publishes a little newspaper, *End Times - Whidbey*, that's a wretched mess of extremist ideas from all over the country – anti-Jewish, anti-Black, anti-Asian, anti-Indian, anti-gay, anti-U.N., anti-government. I can't imagine why anyone takes him seriously. He reminisces a lot about his past glories and seems to have readers all over the country. Many of the articles are just appeals for money to continue his work, and a hodgepodge of stories he picks up from right-wing publications. He's always been careful not to break the law personally, but offers gentle encouragement to those who might have the temperament to do so."

"Sounds a bit like that preacher in northern Idaho who had the neo-Nazi compound."

"Exactly, but that guy was a brighter bulb. Buckley gives them a place to come together on the island and some philosophical support – he 'pretties up' intolerance under the banner of religion and says what they're doing is God's work. Buckley and his hate newspaper will fade away soon, but the game-changer is the heir-apparent, his son Jerry, who has now come onto the scene. Jerry is Internet-savvy and knows his way around Facebook and social media. And he's more inclined to push the envelope."

"What is the scope of Jerry's activities?"

"Jerry's the one we're really watching," Shane says. He explains that with the rise of social media, Jerry has taken the effort beyond a physical newspaper. He communicates in real time with like-minded people across the country. "He airs a weekly live broadcast on

Facebook with thousands of followers. Dresses up in a paramilitary uniform for the camera and the whole bit. Plus, of course, he takes advantage of YouTube, Twitter, Instagram and all the rest. He paints a picture of the Buckley compound as kind of a military fortress and sanctuary for the alt-right."

In the dim predawn, Brad's eye picks out several white highlights in a treetop on the bluff to their right. He counts three shapes and is pretty sure they are Bald Eagles – the national symbol. This looks like a mature pair with white heads and tails, and an immature offspring that hasn't yet developed the white head.

Of course this beach would attract eagles with all the decomposing fish parts, clams, crabs, and other marine life.

The beach is so peaceful on this early morning, Brad wonders how anyone in such a wholesome place finds the time and inclination to hate. He knows most do not. They are simply content to live amid peace and beauty, in a nourishing community where people look out for one another.

But a few find their sense of purpose among self-declared outsiders on the fringes of society. They feel drawn to groups where they can be insiders in semi-secret societies that invoke a bit of the occult or mystic, such as the KKK with its white robes and hoods. In hating, they find some meaning for their disappointing lives.

*

Ray Cobb drifts between waking and sleeping. His mind travels back to when he was a little boy listening to the buzzing of cicadas through the window screen on a sultry Midwest evening. His dad's truck is in the driveway. It's late – he doesn't know how late. The truck door slams with a thunk and then the screen door whaps. A bottle hits the kitchen floor and rolls.

"Where is that little slut?" he hears his dad slur.

"No. Don't you lay a hand on that girl," his mom protests.

Something bounces off the wall.

"Are you . . . are you tellin' me what I can and cannot do in my own home?"

"You've been drinking. Leave her alone. Take it out on me if you must."

"You dried up . . ."

Cobb hears a sickening slap and a groan, and the sound of something hitting the floor.

Heavy footfalls come down the hall and his dad goes into the his sister's room and slams the door.

"Wake up, girlie," Cobb hears.

The next day Cobb's dad digs a hole behind the mobile home. He doesn't say why and the little boy never sees what goes into it. Sometimes his dad buries garbage – bottles and cans.

After that his mother and sister are gone. He assumes his mother left and took his sister with her. He hates his mother for never protecting him from his dad's belt, and for leaving him behind when she goes away. He wants to find his sister, but doesn't know how.

*

Brad's thoughts drift all the way back to a big kid in his school and some memories he wishes he could change.

"Hey, it's the beaner!" the big killed yelled. "Beaner, beaner, beaner!"

The big kid jumped up from his seat on the school bus and pushed the smaller kid hard from behind. He went flying off balance and landed in a heap in the aisle, dropping his lunch bag as he went. The big kid pounced on the bag.

"Lose something?" he called from behind, waving the bag over his head from side to side. Then he tossed it out the open window as the smaller boy picked himself up from the floor.

"Are you going to cry now? Do you need your mama?"

The memory haunts Brad. He realizes, now, he should have stood up for Pablo and come to his defense.

The bully, David, made Pablo his personal project, hounding him on the playground and everywhere he went. Pablo was a mama's boy, a bit simple, and walked with a limp. He struggled to spi-, spi-, spit out a word. None of the popular kids talked to him because if they did, he would latch on like a starving person and never let go.

The popular kids avoided eye contact with him. It was easier to walk past Pablo on the playground, pretend they didn't see him.

Unlike the kids who lived in the better parts of town, Pablo and his mother lived in an old travel trailer by the river. Brad's parents said the mother cleaned and cared for sick old people. They supposed Pablo's limp was from polio. He didn't come to school some days and Brad couldn't blame him.

Kids learn early in life what it's like to be bullied. Sometimes it's easier to be the bully's friend than his enemy.

Brad's class had only one black kid. When somebody yelled "jigaboo" from the school bus, somebody else said it was the bully who did it. But he denied it, said it was a lie, and that it was Pablo. Several kids agreed it wasn't the bully but Pablo, so the bully got away with it.

Brad wonders where the bully is now, all these years later? Maybe in prison or someplace like the Buckley compound with other misfits and outcasts still trying to do something big to say, "Hey, look at me."

He struggles to understand how Shane's ex-wife, Judy, ended up in the company of men so totally different: the steady, straight-arrow cop on the one hand, and Jerry Buckley on the other. He supposes both men were attracted by her whisper-soft voice, blonde hair and sexy ways; he can see how she draws second looks. She's a born flirt. Shane has told Brad he asked her many times during their marriage not to go out in revealing tops and short skirts, but she craved reinforcement from other men that she was attractive.

It would be easy to dismiss her as shallow, a disastrous life partner for someone of Shane's solid temperament. But marriages usually start with high hopes on both sides and he believes that was true of theirs, at least for a while. Brad is quick to allow that, for all of Judy's shortcomings, she is a devoted mom to Billy.

Maybe in Jerry Buckley, Judy saw an exciting man with a hungry appetite and a certainty of purpose that was strongly appealing until she recognized the depth of the darkness that lay in his soul and in the people around him.

"You're mighty quiet," Shane remarks at length.

"What?" Brad replies. "Oh, deep in my own thoughts. I drifted all the way back to childhood, working myself into a terrible state. Tell me again," Brad asks, "what's the connection between the Buckleys and this bank robber the feds caught here on the island all those years ago?"

"Well that incident created a very useful martyr for the cause locally. It gave the Buckleys an excuse to hold annual rallies and invite like-minded people here from all over the country. If you hold a rally and attract counter-protesters, you get on TV. Any conflict is golden publicity to them. The Buckleys' profile in the supremacist movement, which was never that great, suddenly became much higher. That's how it works."

"It's a shame."

"All of it. It's ironic that these movements actually got a boost from the election of a black president a few years ago. You would think just the opposite, but that particular development drove them crazy. It was their worst nightmare. They could do nothing but attempt to delegitimize him as a foreigner ineligible to hold office, even though that was totally false. Of course, we know who fanned the flames of that particular lie for the longest time."

Brad smiles. Lying is almost a point of pride with the guy who holds the office now. When the black president's term ended, the white bully replaced him, a chronic liar. It was as if nothing mattered in politics any more, least of all truth.

Brad looks up at the high bluff on their right. A trickle of sand snakes its way down the steep slope to the rocky beach below. "This bluff is eroding right now as we stand here," he says.

"It's an active feeder bluff," Shane agrees, "constantly eroding. These steep bluffs are the reason many of the beaches on Whidbey are so sandy – they're constantly feeding the shore."

"Nothing stays the same. The irony," Brad says, going back to their conversation, "is that while the current president stirs up hate and fear against people of color, the real threat to America is internal – from white nationalists and those who think we need a revolution. Latinos and Muslims aren't the problem. Since nine-eleven, far more Americans have been killed by home-grown, right-wing extremists than by Islamic terrorists."

"Unfortunately that's true," Shane agrees. "Those of us in law enforcement now have to go up against assault weapons. We face insane people, criminals and supremacists, even children in some cases, whose firepower is greater than ours because it's so easy now for the public to get military-style weapons that were built for war, not personal protection."

"Is that what you think the Buckleys are up to," Brad asks, "massing weapons for something they intend to do?"

"We don't know. We can't prove anything, but if trouble is

going to start on this island, there's a good chance it'll start in the Buckley compound."

"What would the target be?" Brad asks. "Are there any high-value targets on the island?"

"Not really. Not unless you consider the Navy, and that never made sense to me. They maintain pretty high security. I think any troublemaker would look for either a soft target or a symbol of federal enforcement, not the military."

Brad imagines there are plenty of soft targets in the area, everything from progressive churches to ferryboats to minority schools, minority-owned businesses, even liberal universities and facilities that carry out government research. Not to mention oil refineries, if someone wanted to strike a blow against corporate America.

As they stand and talk, Brad watches a large containership glide by, inbound with cargo for Seattle or Tacoma, most likely. It reminds him that for years Homeland Security worried that foreign terrorists would place a dirty bomb in a shipping container bound for an urban port facility. Maybe the real threat now is that domestic terrorists might try it to create chaos and panic.

He imagines this ship carries everything from athletic shoes to TV sets. It catches the first rays of sunrise as they break over the Cascade Mountains. Behind the containership, the Olympic Mountains rise dramatically across the water. Brad feels like he can just about reach out and touch those peaks. He imagines that in the winter, when they're covered with new snow, they must look like the Himalayas.

"Think we can get over that way while Irene and I are here?" Brad asks, nodding toward the mountains.

"Absolutely. You shouldn't go back without getting up in the mountains and paying a visit to Hurricane Ridge."

They walk on, alone with their thoughts till Brad clears his throat.

"There was something I was going to ask you," he begins.

"Yeah?"

"Do you ever dream about Bella?"

Shane looks at Brad sideways a moment, with raised eyebrows and a cocked head. "Not anymore. Not since I married Elizabeth."

"You're a good man."

"Do you?"

Brad casts his eyes down. "I'm afraid so."

"That's not good for you and Irene."

"No."

Shane nods and they walk some more.

"Is it the island?" Shane asks. "Being back here where she died?"

"I'm sure that's part of it. She feels very close here. I can't stop thinking about her."

Shane lets the comment sit a moment. "I'll tell you what I do think about."

"What's that?"

"Bella had such a razor sharp sense of right and wrong, I'm glad she didn't live to see what's happening now – the breakdown of this country into warring camps, with each having its own set of facts. She'd be right in the middle of it, fighting for truth."

"The struggle never ends," Brad says. "It just keeps re-emerging in some new shape."

"That's why I became a cop, you know, and you became a journalist, to keep the darkness at bay."

"And somehow," Brad says, "as dark as things sometimes seem, this looks like the beginning of a beautiful day."

Chapter 9

Billy is just getting up from the table as Brad and Shane come up the front steps and enter the inn. Moose runs ahead and jumps into Billy's arms. Marie is setting out plates and silverware.

Brad proceeds to the kitchen and studies the offerings laid out on the counter – hot platters of scrambled eggs, bacon, sausage and hash browns, plus blueberry waffles, grapefruit and oatmeal.

"You don't eat like this all the time do you, Shane?" he asks.

"Only on special occasions. Elizabeth is used to cooking for our paying guests. This group doesn't pay as well but it's a lot more fun, and it's definitely a special occasion to be with our best friends in the world."

Elizabeth calls after the disappearing boy, "If you're done, Billy, would you check the suet feeder? The birds have just about wiped us out again." She nods toward the feeding station in the front yard. Billy walks to the pantry, opens the cupboard and pulls out two cakes of suet.

Brad watches him unwrap them and go out to the feeder. A chickadee clings to the suet feeder and refuses to take flight till Billy reaches up to unhook the holder. He drops the suet cakes into the holder, rehangs it and returns to the house.

"This is high season for the birds," Shane remarks. "We've got all our tropical migratory birds now and they're already sitting on eggs. As the new broods fledge from the nest, they all come down to the feeder to load up on quick energy."

"We had Western Tanagers already this morning," Billy says, "both the male and female. They like the suet with the dried insects in it."

"Point them out to me, will you?" Brad asks. "Next time you

see them."

He turns to Elizabeth. "This place really seems right for you."

"It is. I've never felt so happy and content. I knew when we found it that it's where my soul belongs."

Brad is glad Shane's dreams don't wander the way his own do. He thinks back to his rule about taking something bad and making it into something good. He and Irene met Elizabeth in the darkest hour of her life, after her brother's murder, only to introduce her to the man who would soon become her husband. Today she seems the happiest she's ever been.

It all happened because Brad and Irene had gone to Elizabeth home to offer condolences. They had been with her brother on the Alaska Ferry when murderers threw him overboard. In the aftermath of that loss, Brad and Irene invited Elizabeth to visit them in Idaho. That's where they introduced her to their divorced detective friend Shane.

Now, Shane and Elizabeth are starting a new life together in this idyllic setting with Shane's son Billy. It's a storybook ending, Brad thinks, and he hopes it's really only the beginning for them.

As for himself, well, then there are other stories that just need an ending.

After breakfast, Brad, Shane and Robert clear the table and load the dishwasher while the women and Billy go for a walk. Shane waits till they're out the door, then announces, "Come into my study, will you both? I have something to show you."

Brad and Robert follow Shane down the hall to his office. He shovels some stacks of paper off two chairs and gestures for Brad and Robert to sit where they can view the screen.

"I loaded the pictures Robert and I took at the rally the other day, including some screen shots from Robert's video." He scrolls through several images. Most of these guys, the ones we can identify, are the usual suspects from Washington, Idaho and Oregon.

"But," he adds, stopping on a close-up of two men talking with Jerry Buckley, ". . . these guys caught my eye," Shane says, "so I ran their pictures through the FBI's facial recognition database."

"And?" Robert asks.

"The one on the left is an ex-Marine, Raymond Cobb of Arkansas. And the one on the right is Fred Franks of Indiana."

"Is that significant?" Robert asks.

"Cobb is a former Marine sharpshooter. He was drummed out of the service after repeated disciplinary incidents, culminating in a vicious assault on his lieutenant. He's short-tempered with no impulse control."

"A sweetheart," Robert mutters.

"Franks is more complex and interesting in some ways – soft spoken and low key. More of a behind-the-scenes guy. He has a series of arrests for bomb making. He's never done anything big, never killed or injured anyone, but has developed some pretty creative improvised explosives. He's served time in prison for counterfeiting and belonged to the Aryan Brotherhood on the inside. In fact that's where Cobb and Franks met – in prison."

"They definitely fit the profile of people who would be inclined toward carrying out something big," Brad says.

"They do," Shane agrees. "I don't think they traveled all the way from the Midwest just to carry signs in a little demonstration on Whidbey Island."

Robert leans closer to the computer and stares intently at the photo of Cobb. "That's the guy who called me a half-breed and said I should go back to the reservation."

When Robert sits back in his chair, Brad takes his own turn studying the photos. The bald-headed Cobb is all bulging muscles, built like a fire hydrant. Brad sees barely suppressed anger in those eyes. Franks looks disarmingly normal and thoughtful, almost professorial. Harder to read.

"There's something else," Shane says. He types some more keys on his computer and opens a photo archive of images taken at the gate of the Buckley compound. Brad recognizes the same two men in several photographs of vehicles entering the compound. The images are date-stamped as recently as yesterday.

"How much can you see inside the compound?" Robert asks.

"We've done some drone photography but it tells us only so much. We have to fly high so they don't catch us at it. We can't get down low and look through windows. And also, we can't keep a drone in the air all the time – only for short periods when we can spare someone to fly it."

"I was just going to ask about that," Brad interjects.

Robert stares at the images. "How do these guys support themselves to finance their travel out to Washington and whatever neo-Nazi activities they may be up to?"

"Neither one has a work history beyond the military and odd jobs, and prison time with all expenses paid," Shane replies, smiling. "Cobb has done some construction labor and Franks worked in a warehouse. It's a pretty good bet that Jerry Buckley is bankrolling their stay at the compound. He's raking in donations from his live broadcasts on Facebook and other social media."

"Any sign that Judy might be at the compound?" Robert asks.

"We were hoping to get a sighting of her, but so far there's just one thing that might or might not be significant." Shane pushes some more keys and displays several grainy images of a stocky woman crossing the compound with what appears to be a tray. The time stamps on all the photographs correspond with mealtimes.

"Who's the woman?" Brad asks.

"Buford Boh's wife, Ida Rae."

"How did you get these?" he asks.

"From the drone pretty high up. That's why they aren't sharper."

Brad looks up.

Shane continues, "We think she might be taking meals to someone who's detained there. I'm trying not to get my hopes up too much but I'd like to believe Judy is either staying there of her own accord or being held there. One thing we can see clearly is that the Buckleys have surveillance cameras all over the place." He punches up a wider aerial photograph on the computer. "See," he says, "here, here and here. And someone is always patrolling the grounds."

"Pretty extensive," Robert says, studying the image.

"That would be Jerry's doing," Shane continues. "He's brought his dad's security system into the Twenty-first Century. In hindsight the old watchtower is rather quaint and charming. Even if we could get someone inside the grounds, it would be hard to move around without showing up on one of those cameras. We suspect they have infrared sensors as well."

"Could you cut the power?" Robert asks. "You know, create one of those Whidbey Island power outages you talk about?"

"They've got generator backup for everything."

"Well here's a question," Brad begins. "If Jerry Buckley is planning something big with these militants, do you think his dad is part of it?"

"I've wondered about that. It's hard to believe he wouldn't know. But on the other hand, Buford Boh is getting up in years and he's tired, in poor health, getting down toward the end. He's spent his whole life stirring up religious and racial divisions, putting down people who don't look like him, but has never done anything specifically against the law that I know of. It's a lot easier to picture Jerry taking direct action than his dad, who probably just wants to live out his remaining time in peace."

"So what's our plan for now?" Brad asks.

"We've got a lot of eyes and ears on alert all over the island – sheriff's department, FBI, state patrol, Langley and Oak Harbor police, ferry system and Navy. That's about all we can do till we can pick up Judy's trail or spot some activity that raises concern. In the meantime, we go ahead with business as usual. As far as the department is concerned I'm on vacation for your visit. But you know, I work under the radar a lot. My brain can't let go."

"I know," Brad says. "Neither can mine."

*

Brad, Irene and Elizabeth thread their way among tourists on Langley's Anthes Avenue, past the whale museum, barbershop and thrift store to the corner of Second Street.

"Oh, that's the church," Irene remarks, "where you took Marie and me for the immigrant potluck."

"Yes," Elizabeth replies. "I wanted Brad to see it, too."

"Irene told me about the potluck – said it was pretty emotional."

Everyone in the world, he believes, wants the same thing – a better life for their children. Perhaps for one brief moment in this social hall, where strangers treat them as friends, they can imagine what that life could be.

Irene remarks that the people she saw at the church didn't look like fanatics and terrorists. The older generation were dressed in suits and better clothes, and seemed to be retired business people and professionals. The children seemed surprisingly typical of American kids, full of enthusiasm and curiosity. They kept busy with crayons and colored pencils.

Irene adds that the group's interpreter explained that most of this group came here to join other family members or relatives who emigrated to this country before them. They are starting over with nothing because they lost everything they owned, and all of their savings, in the bombing and destruction at home."

Brad can't imagine any place more different from the bombed-out ruins of Aleppo than the seaside village of Langley. It's a charmed place in every respect. He realizes most of the world is not as wholesome as this, though he thinks his own community of Stanley, Idaho, has the same general character and warm people, albeit in a Wild West setting. Langley and Stanley both have crime and social problems, of course, but not a lot. Both have a well-educated populace, surprisingly diverse, and a rich cultural and creative community.

Elizabeth leads Brad and Irene up Second Street, past the Star Store grocery, a restaurant, two coffee houses and the post office, to city hall.

Brad notes that the town's seat of government is a handsome, older, two-story brick building.

"Like much of Langley," Elizabeth points out, "City Hall is quaint and picturesque. What surprised us was to discover that the elected representatives have some fairly wide political and philosophical differences, as we learned during the city council debate about making Langley a sanctuary city."

"So that was a sore point," Brad remarks.

"Yeah. We had no idea city government had moved to the right as far as it has."

The group walks on, past the library to the high bluff on Cascade Avenue, overlooking the town's boat harbor, and facing across at Everett and the full panorama of Cascade Mountains peaks.

"This is stunning," Brad remarks.

"Speaking of immigrants," Elizabeth points out, "the town's founder, was a young German immigrant. He chose this spot for a homestead and town site, and made his livelihood harvesting firewood for the Puget Sound steamships, to keep the ships' boilers going." Up until the 1930s when Deception Pass Bridge was built, water transportation was the only way to get to Whidbey and a lot of other places around the sound. And it didn't hurt that the town's setting was breathtakingly beautiful.

The group doubles back to First Street where Elizabeth points out the pizzeria, bookstore, movie house and several restaurants, galleries and tourist shops.

"It's everything you could ask for in a small town," Brad observes.

"All about an hour from the high-rise office towers of Seattle," Elizabeth adds.

Brad already knows he's going to write about this for his commentary on public radio. There is a powerful, compelling story in what's happening on this island that has such a romantic, idyllic reputation in the eyes of many. He's not sure how it's going to play out. But by the time he leaves this place, he's going to have a story.

*

Judy awakens naked on her back, pinned in that position with Jerry's arm sprawled across her chest. She wonders if he did it deliberately. Jerry lies on his side, facing her, snoring. Her bladder is full and she needs the bathroom. She tries to lift his arm without awakening him, but he stirs, so she gently pushes on his shoulder.

"I need to get up," she whispers.

"What?"

"I need to pee."

"What? Ok."

Judy climbs over him and heads for the toilet. When she comes out, she looks for her T-shirt on the floor and doesn't find it. She scans the darkness for his gun. She'd like to look through his pants and coat for his keys, but in the darkness she can't tell if his eyes are open or closed. She doesn't dare make a move if he's half awake. Then he would know then that she's only pretending to play along.

She finds the switch for an under-cabinet light. She scoops some coffee into the basket of the coffeemaker, fills the carafe and starts the machine. She's stalling a bit, buying time to think, giving him time to drift off. The machine starts to gurgle.

When she turns around she feels a chill. His eyes are staring straight at her. She takes a few steps and they follow her in the dim light. Is he watching her body or her hands? She climbs back on top of bed with him as the aroma of coffee fills the room. Jerry's eyes shift toward the far end of the bed.

What is he looking at?

"Don't look at my toes!" Judy screams.

"Why?" Jerry asks, startled. "What's wrong? I have this thing about feet."

"Mine are ugly!" Judy replies. "Don't look at them!"

"Ok, ok. Not looking at them. Jesus."

He puts his arm around her, pulls her closer, and they lie there.

"I feel like you're freezing me out of whatever's going on," Judy declares, wrapping her legs around him.

"Mmmmft. What?"

"Whatever it is, let me help. I know something's up and it has to do with those two guys you're spending so much time with, the nice man and the scary man."

"Not going to happen."

"You're not going to tell me? You're wasting my talent, keeping me penned up in this compound with your mother when I could be helping you."

"Talent?" Jerry laughs. "Seriously?"

"I can go places the rest of you can't and I can be useful," she says, batting her eyes. "Nobody suspects a pretty girl," she says, tossing her long mane and making a flirtatious face. "I'm not one of those tattooed biker women who screams Nazi."

"Be thankful you're not involved."

"Why?"

"It's complicated."

"It can't be that complicated."

Jerry's expression is pained. "This is some serious shit," he says. "It's better if you stay out of it. And honestly, I don't know you that well anyway. Nobody does."

The remark shocks her.

"How can you say that? You haven't given me a chance. But apparently you know me well enough to screw me."

"That's a different issue."

"It's not an 'issue' to me. It's my body."

"It's not just up to me, ok? People have to know they can trust you."

"What people?"

"Certain people with a lot to lose."

"It's those guys, isn't it? Let me talk to them."

"Be careful what you wish for," Jerry says. "Keep as far away from them as you can. You're about this close to being in a landfill," he says, extending his fingers an inch apart. "They want you gone. I'm doing you a favor."

Judy just stares, wide-eyed.

"What do I have to do to prove you can trust me?"

"Just sit tight. Don't ask any questions. You're alive so far; that's something. I don't even know if I'm safe with these two."

Chapter 10

From the car deck of the MV Kennewick, Brad watches the shore fall away as the ferry pulls out of Keystone Harbor on its way to Port Townsend. The acceleration is smooth and he almost doesn't realize they are under way. He wonders about all the big trucks lined up in front of Shane's Suburban. Any one of them could be carrying a bomb.

The Suburban was the last vehicle to board and is parked at the end of the tunnel – the boat's central vehicle bay. Ahead of them are an 18-wheeler, a diesel motor home, an empty logging truck, several box trucks, a hippie van, two teardrop campers and a truckload of mussels. The ferry clears the tiny harbor, churning white froth in its wake, and accelerates for the half-hour crossing of Admiralty Inlet to Port Townsend.

"There isn't much security on this crossing, is there?" Brad asks. "I didn't see any police screening or bomb-sniffing dogs in the holding area. I expected the state patrol or other uniformed officers."

"No," Shane says. "The cross-sound run isn't as heavily traveled as Mukilteo-Clinton, which carries a lot more foot passengers. I think on this run the crew is mostly responsible for security. These boats are smaller than the ones on the Mukilteo run and carry fewer passengers. The high-profile Mukilteo crossing carries a lot of Boeing commuters and people headed to downtown Seattle."

Boeing. That's another good target, Brad thinks.

"I thought the ferries and other mass transportation systems came under tighter scrutiny after nine eleven," Brad says as they climb the stairs to the passenger deck and head back to the outside railing at the stern, where there's some shelter from the wind generated by the ship's speed.

"They did, but the state prioritizes resources according to the perceived threat, and with fewer passengers this particular run isn't in the same category as the more heavily traveled routes serving urban areas such as Seattle, especially."

As the ferry emerges from the little harbor, Brad gets his first look back at Admiralty Head and the concrete bulwarks of Fort Casey. The sky is deep blue on this summer morning and he watches a few early walkers with a dog explore the sandy beaches at the foot of the bluff.

Shane points out that back in the late 1800s when it was easier to tell the difference between friends and enemies, Fort Casey was one of three army forts with mortars and big guns guarding the entrance of Puget Sound from hostile navies. The other two are visible across the way, he says, turning and pointing toward two low-lying areas on the Port Townsend side, "Fort Worden and Fort Flagler."

Brad thinks it's ironic that the threats used to be from conventional armies and navies, symbolized by these old forts that are relics. Now the greatest threat to American lives is from homegrown terrorists and self-declared patriots acting individually or in small cells.

"We are lucky that all three of these forts are in the state park system now," Shane says, "and are preserved for the public for camping, concerts, marine labs and beaches."

While the women and Billy head for the passenger cabin, the three men stay out on the deck to soak up the sunshine and marine air. "Don't you love this atmosphere?" Brad asks. "Sort of a mixture of salt and seaweed, I guess. It's pleasant." A few gulls follow the boat, squawking and criss-crossing their wake. Someone at the stern railing is holding French fries at arm's length and the braver birds are swooping down and grabbing them in flight.

In the distance, Brad watches a sailboat tack north toward the Strait of Juan de Fuca. Nearby, a tug tows a gravel barge south.

"This run takes us right across the shipping lanes," Shane remarks. "Aircraft carriers, nuclear submarines, containerships – everything entering Puget Sound passes this way. There's a lot of Navy activity at Indian Island," he says, "tucked just inside Marrowstone Island." He points toward some large cranes in the distance. "That's where the Navy stores a quarter of the nation's nuclear munitions for the Trident submarines."

Robert takes it all in. "There's no shortage of important facilities," he says.

"That whole island is a network of concrete bunkers," Shane says. "The challenge is to get inside the thinking of a terrorist group and imagine how they would assess the opportunities if they wanted to target it."

"In the past," Brad points out, "haven't they focused mostly on targets symbolic of federal law enforcement and on minority groups, such as Jewish community centers?"

"That's true," Shane agrees.

"Even my wife is a target," Robert says, "as a federal law enforcement officer. Some of these anti-government types don't like laws regulating where and when they can hunt, and the agents who enforce them."

As they talk, Shane starts to edge toward the cabin, prodding them toward the bow for a better view of the old brick buildings of Port Townsend as the ferry approaches. As they pass through the cabin, they find the women and Billy hunched over a crossword puzzle. Marie, Elizabeth and Billy get up and follow the men, leaving Irene holding a puzzle piece in mid air, still looking for where it might fit.

Billy is first to spot what is right next to the boat.

"Right there!" he yells, pointing off to the side. "In the water." A curious, whiskered face watches them pass as it bobs in the water a few feet from the boat.

"What is it?" Marie asks.

"A harbor seal," Billy replies. Seabirds float in a cluster nearby, paddling and occasionally diving. A few fishermen and their boats dot the water here, in what looks to be a rip current just offshore.

Brad's eye is on the Victorian architecture of town. In his imagination it takes him back more than a century to when Port Townsend was a booming city, a boat-building center and shipment point for logs and lumber from peninsula mills. He wonders how those old buildings will do in an earthquake.

Shane explains, "Port Townsend was the jumping off point for the earliest travelers to Whidbey Island. The boat ran to Ebey's Landing, where livestock were pushed overboard to swim ashore, and where people and cargo got into smaller boats to run up on the beach."

"Wasn't there an inn for travelers at Ebey's Landing?" Brad asks.

"Yes, people waiting for the ferry on the Whidbey side often spent the night at the Ferry House, just a short walk from the beach. It's still there, preserved as a historic site now," Shane says.

He adds that he has toured the inside of the Ferry House on special occasions when it's been open to the public. It's possible to see patches of the original wallpaper and worn treads on the stairway, rounded by decades of boots trudging up and down those stairs. There are several brick fireplaces, and it's not hard to imagine men in the parlor, smoking their cigars and pipes as they catch up on the news from other travelers.

"The settlers' problems were very different then," Brad observes, "worrying about crops and disease, and raiding parties of natives."

"We're just coming into the landing," Robert remarks as the engine goes quiet and the boat begins to glide. "Maybe we'd better get back to the car."

Brad lingers a moment to soak up the still morning. Handsome Victorian homes line the rim of the bluff above. A few cars pass by on the main street, entering and leaving the downtown area, which is mostly to the right.

Finally he turns and follows the rest of the group back to the car.

An hour later, they pass through Sequim and Port Angeles, and start to climb the winding road to Hurricane Ridge in Olympic National Park. The two-lane road hugs the hillside on the right and steep canyons on the left. They stop for deer trotting along the narrow shoulder. Lush evergreens ripple across the landscape in waves of blue and green. Above them, the view is of rocky, snow-covered crags and glaciers. At the first highway pullout, Brad looks all the way back at their route to Port Angeles and the blue expanse of the Strait of Juan de Fuca.

"Over this way," Shane explains, "you can make out Whidbey Island and Mount Baker, which looms large in the distance, near the Canadian border."

"Those Cascade volcanoes really stand out when you see them

from this perspective," Brad remarks.

Marie, who is holding baby Martin in her arms, remarks, "There's so much beauty in this part of the country, and so much space."

*

In the barn, Ray Cobb leads Fred Franks and Jerry Buckley to the back of the box truck. Cobb rolls up the cargo door and pulls out the loading ramp, then walks up the incline into the bay. Jerry looks up at the cargo area, which is filled with an industrial-size, dark green, plastic tank.

Cobb taps the wall of the tank and gets a resonant, deep echo from inside.

"Two-thousand, one hundred gallons," he declares, patting its wall. "Designed for water storage or industrial spraying."

"And you got this where?" Jerry asks.

"Off island, from a farm store in rural King County. I paid cash."

"You stayed off the ferry?"

"Right. Drove around on the back roads, across Deception Pass."

"So none of this is traceable back to the island?"

"None of it. Not us. Not the truck. Not the water tank."

"What about the ammonium nitrate?" Jerry asks, pointing toward the shed behind the barn where a large stack of bags is piled out of the weather.

"From three different farm stores on the mainland," Franks says. "The entire amount is about what a farmer would apply to a few acres of cropland, so there's no reason for anyone even to wonder about it."

"That stuff is horrible by the way," Jerry says. "Stinks to high heaven."

"That's why we stacked the bags out in the shed," Franks says. "For some air circulation. It's the fumes -- damned toxic."

"This is going to be heavy when you fill it," Jerry remarks. "Didn't Tim McVeigh do his mixing in barrels, about forty of them?"

"This is better," Franks replies. "This is going to be much easier and we'll mix it all in the truck, out of sight."

"What about you, Ray?" Jerry asks. "Do you have what you need?"

Ray nods. He steps into a nearby horse stall and pushes back a pile of hay with his boot till he uncovers a blanket. He peels back the corner to reveal a sinister, black weapon that looks like something from Star Wars. Jerry stares at it for a moment before Ray puts back the blanket and pushes the hay over it.

"What is that?"

Ray laughs. "Grenade launcher. Souvenir of my military career."

"What the hell is that for?" Jerry asks.

"It's the detonator," Ray says, fixing a stare on Jerry before breaking into a hearty laugh. Jerry can't quite tell if Cobb is serious or just pulling his leg.

Franks asks, "Does your dad know what we're up to out here?"

"No. He's aware we're working on something big to surprise the feds but I think he actually prefers not knowing the details. He can't be responsible for what he doesn't know. I've kept him out of it."

"Good. The fewer people who know, the better," Cobb says. "And speaking of that, have you taken care of the little problem we talked about?"

"The girl?" Jerry replies. He pauses before adding, "Working on it. What happens when this is over?"

"Nobody sees Fred or me again," Cobb says. "You go back to Bible study and womanizing, minus one pupil."

If only it were that simple. In theory, this scenario sounds nice and tidy, Jerry thinks, but in reality it's more complicated. He really doesn't have the appetite for murder – especially not killing Judy – but it seems there's no way around it. Franks and Cobb are set on it, and Cobb is not only ruthless but cruel. Jerry didn't foresee this when he invited the men out here at the same time he started dating his sexy girlfriend – didn't realize what this would mean for her.

But Jerry knows if he doesn't get rid of her soon, Cobb will do the job and enjoy it. Whether Cobb will be satisfied to stop with Judy's death or arrange Jerry's own disappearance as well, he's no longer sure. He senses he hasn't impressed Cobb with his foot-dragging. The original idea on Jerry's part was to incite a race war and take some credit for it. Becoming a victim of "friendly fire" in the process is not what Jerry had in mind, but it's clear his accomplices intend to cover their tracks.

In hindsight, Jerry's dad, Buford Boh, had a surprisingly good run in the supremacist business without directly breaking the law. It's easy to talk tough, to give rousing speeches and be a big shot like his dad, write letters to the newspaper and wave signs at parades. His dad always knew how to walk up to the edge but not step over it. With the social media, Jerry realizes, it can be harder not to take things too far.

To become the next Timothy McVeigh would be heady stuff. But Jerry knows McVeigh paid the price for that when he went to the execution chamber.

The reality, Jerry realizes, is that if any of the three conspirators gets caught someday for any reason and decides to bargain with the feds, the other two are going to jail. Three can keep a secret, but only if two are dead.

The kicker, Jerry is pretty sure, is that Franks and Cobb are thinking the same thing. He wonders how much cleanup each of them may be planning, unknown to the others.

He wishes he could walk this back a few steps. He's increasingly worried they can't pull this off without it being traced back to the compound. McVeigh's partner, Terry Nichols, bowed out at the last minute and saved his own skin, though he's now serving one hundred sixty one consecutive life terms. Jerry realizes he's already implicated so deeply in this plot he is totally screwed. Nothing can save him now.

This whole idea, Jerry recalls, goes back about three months to a conversation he had with Cobb in a chat room. To be taken seriously by a prominent militant was exhilarating. Jerry said he was tired of empty talk – he was ready to do something that would make a difference.

Cobb asked if he really meant it. Jerry said yes and Cobb said. "We'll talk more. I know a guy you should meet."

Jerry invited Cobb and his friend out to the rally.

Now he wonders which of the three conspirators will still be standing when this is over. His shirt feels wet and he smells the odor of sweat. His armpits are soaked.

*

Judy can't stop thinking about the beating. It was sickening and apparently administered for no good reason, based on Jerry's remark to the bald-headed guy he called Ray. Jerry said that the victim, "didn't mean anything." Ray was the driver of the box truck that arrived at the compound two days ago and was quickly backed out of sight in the barn. Ray seemed to be someone important, and also someone you didn't cross.

Judy hasn't seen the victim since then, the man Jerry drove to the hospital, but Ray and another guy have been coming and going from the barn. Jerry, too.

She's also seen other men making deliveries to the compound. They come at night and often in pickup trucks with what looks like feed sacks in the back. It's a lot of activity. Judy wonders if the box truck has something to do with all this other activity that also seems to center on the barn.

Judging by the pattern, they are working on something very important inside, out of sight. She suspects they are close to completing whatever it is. When that happens, then what? Will they be done with her, too?

*

Oblivious to crowds of people, deer graze the grassy alpine slopes of Hurricane Ridge. After a leisurely drive to the summit on the Heart of the Hills Highway, Shane's group finds the parking area almost as busy as a small city. Brad catches bits of conversation in German and Japanese. As the crowd basks in radiant sunshine and shirtsleeves, Shane's guests look across a deep valley at snowfields and glaciers even higher up the next ridge.

"We'll walk around here at the visitor center for a while," Shane says, "then run back to Sequim. I have a favorite local secret to show you and a couple of other surprises."

An hour later, as they pass through downtown Port Angeles on their way back, Brad notices what looks like a gray-and-white passenger liner approaching the city's waterfront. As they watch, the vessel blows its deep whistle to announce its arrival.

Shane points out it's a privately-owned ferry, the MV Coho, which makes several ninety-minute crossings a day from Port Angeles to Victoria, on Canada's Vancouver Island.

Brad remembers reading about this ferry. In 1999, a US Customs inspector in Port Angeles became suspicious when she interviewed the driver of a car arriving from Victoria. The driver's answers seemed a bit off. It was the last car coming off the boat. The inspector made a spot decision to take the extra step of searching the vehicle, and when she opened the trunk she found it loaded with explosives. It turned out the driver was an al-Qaeda terrorist intending to take part in a New Year's Eve attack on Los Angeles Airport.

The incident was a reminder of the difference one officer's instincts can make in thwarting disaster. That one moment of curiosity was probably the single most important decision of her entire career.

It's a quick drive from Port Angeles back to Sequim, where Shane exits the freeway and turns onto a rural lane, past country homes, tidy gardens, horses and small farms. They enter a grove of trees, and the dappled shade is delightful. Brad becomes aware of a river at the roadside, flowing shallowly over rocks and rapids.

"The river is the Dungeness," Shane says, "the second steepest river in the United States, but only thirty-two miles long from its headwaters in the Olympic Mountains to where it enters the Strait of Juan de Fuca."

"It's full of salmon and trout."

"Cool!" Billy exclaims.

"Oh, it's even cooler than that," Shane adds, "because this is Railroad Bridge Park, an old rail bed that's now a trail for walking. You can walk out on the bridge over the river or, someday in the future, follow the Olympic Discovery Trail all the way to the coast. But what I especially want you to see is the Dungeness River Audubon Center here with its taxidermy collection of just about every bird and animal found on the peninsula."

"What a perfect introduction to the Olympic Peninsula," Marie says.

Brad spots some interpretive signs and heads for them, while Billy and Elizabeth follow Robert and Marie into the Audubon Center. Suddenly they're immersed in black bears and river otters, beavers, flying squirrels, hawks, owls and woodpeckers that look lifelike enough to have walked in from the woods.

"We'll take some time to relax and browse here and meet back at the car in an hour," Shane tells the group.

*

"I brought you some reading material," Jerry says as he enters the cabin and plops several magazines and newspapers down on the desk.

Judy paws at the selection – several issues of his dad's newspaper, other right-wing publications, one issue of *People* and one dog-eared copy of *National Geographic*.

Thank god for the *People,* Judy thinks. The magazines are a good sign. If Jerry still cares enough to do this, he hasn't written her off yet. The magazine selection is pathetic but she wraps both arms around him and hugs him hard. He lifts her off her feet and spins her around like a doll. When he puts her down at last, she plasters him with kisses on his lips, neck and ear lobes. His coarse, black beard seems to grow all the way into his ears.

"Damn, girl! Are you trying to get on my good side?"

"I'm just naturally friendly," Judy replies with a bat of the eyelashes. "It pains me to see you go through such a tough time. I don't know what is weighing on you so much or how I can make it better but I'll do anything for you. I love you, babe."

"I know," he says. "I know. Just keep doing what you're doing."

She reaches for the buttons on his shirt and starts opening them. "Would you like a massage? Sit down here in this chair and I'll loosen up your shoulders."

Jerry does as she asks and she works her fingers around his neck and collar area.

"These muscles are tight," Judy declares as she manipulates his shoulders and digs her thumbs into knots on his back. "There's a knot here," she says, pressing so hard Jerry cries out. "You're really tense," she adds. She knows he has a gun. If she could get to it, is there any way she could zip-tie and gag Jerry, and get out of this compound alive?

"I'm under a lot of pressure," he says.

"What's doing this to you, honey?"

"I got myself into a situation. I don't see eye to eye with a couple of guys and can't afford to get on their bad side." As she works, his muscles loosen; he closes his eyes and starts to slump. On the desk beside him, she notices the plastic ends of several objects that are stringy and black – zip ties, she thinks. She's seen them before.

A shiver runs through her. Are the zip ties for someone else or for her?

"Oh man, you are good," Jerry says.

"Relax," she remarks. "Let yourself go. I'm here for you."

*

Brad and Shane lean on the railing of Railroad Bridge and listen to the trickle of water. Beneath the trestle, the river meanders over a broad area of gravel bars in a braid of streams, eddies, pools and back channels. On a gravel bar, a young woman throws a stick for her German Shepherd. A procession of hikers, joggers, bicyclists and walkers of all ages come toward them across the long bridge span.

"Looking at the river right here," Brad begins, "it's hard to imagine it starts so high up in the mountains and, just a few miles later, becomes what we see in front of us."

It strikes Brad as a rare and special place. So many rivers get straightened, dammed and diked for power generation and erosion control, but this one still has a natural flood plain. The river here is free to spread out and slow down in the shallows, and wind its way among gravel bars and around obstacles, trees and stumps. He knows this is just a few miles from saltwater and it's a perfect habitat for spawning chums. This one short river accounts for a sand spit, Ediz Hook, reaching three miles to sea in the Strait of Juan de Fuca.

Trees on both banks lean over the river and shade its banks, their leaves shimmering in the breeze.

"It's relaxing," Brad says, "but I know this isn't a relaxing day for you. Your mind is somewhere else, as it has to be."

"It's hard to feel settled without some word about Judy."

"Has Billy asked why she hasn't called?"

"Ordinarily I think he'd be asking, but he's pretty distracted by your visit so that's a break for now."

"Has your department picked up any indication of what might be brewing at the compound?"

"No and that's a growing worry. Cobb and Franks are hanging

around. The drone is seeing a lot of activity but we don't know what it means. Given the histories of those two men, everyone is on edge."

Chapter 11

It is late afternoon when the Hurricane Ridge travelers roll off the Port Townsend – Coupeville ferry onto Whidbey Island again after their day trip to the peninsula.

"There's someplace Brad and I have to show you," Shane says. "We'll get some dinner there. It holds a lot of memories and I haven't stopped thinking about it since the first time Brad and I met there."

Irene has a feeling this is about Brad's old love, Bella.

Shane turns the big Suburban north from the ferry and keeps going past the exit for Coupeville several miles to Madrona Way, where he turns right.

They drive along the Penn Cove shoreline until she sees a sign for The Captain Whidbey Inn, which rings a bell from Brad's stories. Shane turns up a forested driveway till it ends in a grove of red-barked Madrona trees, where he parks in the shade. They all pile out.

"I love this," Marie says, when she sets eyes on the inn on a low bluff overlooking the water. "What a classic old building. Are those Madrona logs that it's built of? I've never seen that before."

"Let's find a spot outside on the patio," Brad says, leading the group around front and across the lawn.

In the shade of two patio umbrellas they order drinks from the bar, followed by a mixed menu of appetizers, mussels, salads and burgers for the group. The day and the food catch up with them, and soon they are relaxed and mellow.

"This is where Shane and Stu and I really bared our souls with one another about Bella's death," Brad explains. "It was a cat and mouse game with Shane at first. He was thinking Stu and I were a couple of sleazy reporters on the trail of a story, and we were wondering if Shane was involved in a whitewash or a sordid romance."

"I never said you were sleazy," Shane corrects.

"Maybe not those exact words," Brad allows. "And I would never call you sordid. Not now anyway."

"But everyone's a suspect."

"In any case, somehow a partnership and friendship were born," Brad says, "and I think we should toast that friendship and also the new partners who have joined us – Elizabeth, Robert, Marie and Irene."

Everyone raises glasses and they all clink together.

For Brad it's a bittersweet moment – rekindling some of the happiest and saddest memories of his life about Bella and Stu. Now, sitting here this afternoon with his best friends in the world, he wonders if this might be the last time he will be with them. He feels the presence of Bella very close.

"Stu and I did some good talking in this very spot," Brad says, willing Bella out of his mind. "And despite our ups and downs, I miss him terribly."

Everyone murmurs agreement.

Brad smiles, "And darn if he didn't fire a warning shot at me here, too. It was that window right there," Brad adds, pointing to an upstairs room. "Glass sprayed all over the place from the mirror behind me. I was down on my hands and knees, scared out of my wits."

Everyone laughs.

"Shane showed up awfully fast with his gun," Brad adds. "That rattled me even more. I wasn't sure at first whose side he was on – whether he was there to find the shooter or whether he actually *was* the shooter."

*

Judy looks out at the clearing. She watches Jerry having what looks like a stressful discussion with the men, waving his arms. It's the same two who backed the truck into the barn. One of them, the driver's friend, looks almost fatherly and kind. The other one, the driver, wears a mean expression and she has already seen what he's capable of.

These are the men with whom Jerry is having problems – the ones Jerry said want her dumped in a landfill. The vicious one looks her way – glares at the little cabin. He knows exactly where she is. Are they talking about her now? That is not good and she wonders if they'll come for her at some point. She wishes she could read Jerry's thoughts – to know whose side he's on.

On the other hand, Shane will be looking for her by now. He'll be watching Jerry and this compound. The only question is whether Shane realizes how urgently she needs to get out of here.

What would it take, she wonders, to get Jerry's mom to unlock the door?

*

It's evening by the time the travelers get back to Freeland. Elizabeth, Marie and Irene soon settle with Martin and Billy in the front parlor, flipping through Irene's sketchbooks of Idaho wildlife and wildflowers. Billy is interested in sketching birds and Irene promises him a lesson.

Shane's cell phone rings and he steps out of the room to take the call. When he returns several minutes later, he asks Brad and Robert to join him in the den.

"We've got some new developments," he announces. "Because of Fred Franks' history with explosives, just to be thorough, I had an officer canvas farm stores in a fifty-mile radius. Several stores in the Snohomish area sold ammonium nitrate fertilizer this week to cash buyers they hadn't dealt with before. It's the explosive of choice for truck bombs. It may be nothing, but these stores tend to deal with repeat customers, so this pattern stood out. The amounts weren't large, but if you combine them they add up."

"Interesting," Robert says, nodding. "It could be nothing, but then again . . ."

"There's more. Someone in a Budget rental box truck bought a large plastic water tank in Snohomish. Again, he paid cash, which is unusual."

"Do we have a description?" Robert asks.

"Just a general description at this point because the clerk wasn't paying much attention at the time. She called him 'average everything – height, weight, age. Clean-shaven.' Said he was muscular but his skin wasn't as ruddy as most farmers who spend a lot of time outdoors. Oh, and his breath smelled of cigarettes – she really noticed that. She said the guy was not terribly friendly, wouldn't make small talk and didn't want to talk about what he was going to do with the tank."

Brad raises his eyebrows. "That's odd," he says. "What kind of farmer doesn't want to talk about what he's doing and how it's going? Farmers love to complain – about the weather, the harvest, prices."

"The thing is," Shane adds, "Cobb's presumed partner, Franks, is known to be quite an admirer of the Oklahoma City bomber, Tim McVeigh. He has posted on supremacist websites how much he respects McVeigh's resourcefulness and the tight-lipped way he handled himself after he was captured."

"Oh man," Brad groans.

"Yeah, and we also located the rental place where the truck originated. This is the best part. The driver paid a cash deposit and used a driver's license for ID. We checked and determined it was stolen."

"Any idea where the truck is now?" Brad asks.

"Vanished. We're checking traffic cameras to see if we can reconstruct which way it was headed. I know where I'd look if I could, but we don't have any reasonable basis on which to ask a judge to authorize a search warrant of the Buckley compound. "

"Franks is a bomb maker so I can understand what his role might be if they're up to something," Brad says. "But where does Cobb fit into this? Why would Franks or Jerry Buckley need a powder keg like Cobb working with them?"

"I agree," Shane says. "Cobb seems an odd partner to be teamed up with someone as patient and methodical as Franks. Franks is low key. Cobb is short-fused, more of a human powder keg. He's capable of just about anything."

Robert rubs his eyes. "There are enough red flags here. I think we've got to get someone into that compound to look around."

"I don't think we can wait any longer," Shane agrees.

Brad finds his mind drifting as Robert and Shane talk. It's getting harder to keep his eyes open and he finally realizes he's losing the battle to stay awake.

"I think I'm going to have to leave you two to work this out. I'm a little weary after our big day," he announces. "I think I'll turn in early and catch up on my sleep."

Robert and Shane exchange glances and watch Brad disappear down the hallway toward his room.

"That was odd," Shane remarks. "What's going on with him?"

Chapter 12

Blood runs down Marie's leg where she scraped it on a downed tree. She doesn't usually wear shorts any more, and today is the worst possible time for them. She reaches down to see how bad the bleeding is and just succeeds in smearing it all over her leg with the palm of her hand. Robert offers an arm to help her climb over the next log.

"I hurt all over and I'm half drowned from slogging through that wetland," she declares. "My wound hurts, but by god we did it."

She looks down at the scar on her calf where a poacher shot her years ago. She won that fight and arrested him, but the wound aches sometimes when she gets really tired, and it's sure aching now.

"Darn if you don't look even worse than I do," she says as she takes stock of Robert's white legs, which are just as muddy and bloody without the protection of long pants.

"Time to ditch the GPS," Robert says. "We're coming into the clearing." Marie unclips the unit from her belt and tosses it into a clump of salal. Ahead, the forest thins out and Marie can see a cluster of buildings.

"Good navigating, by the way," Robert says. "There's no fence on this side of the compound. The terrain is so bad, no one would even try what we just did."

"Apparently they haven't seen us yet. Based on the drone photography, that looks like the cabin up ahead that Shane wanted us to check – where Ida Mae was taking meals."

"Most of the windows are boarded," Marie says.

"... Which is what you would expect if it's being used as a holding cell," Robert says. "Let's try to get a look inside before they figure out we're here. If we're lucky maybe we can scope out the barn, too."

They reach the back of the cabin and work their way around. At the front, Marie peeks through a window and sees nothing, then continues ahead to the next one with Robert right behind her.

She cranes her head to look inside, then jumps back and turns.

"I think it's Judy," she whispers, "on the bed. I looked right at her but she didn't see me." Marie goes back to the window and taps softly.

Judy stirs slightly, then rolls over and stares at the window. "Marie?" she asks. "Is it really you?" She gets up from the bed and slides the window open. "Marie!" she exclaims. "Oh my god. Am I ever glad to see you. How did you get here?"

"The hard way through the woods and swamp," Marie replies. "We have only minutes before they'll catch us. Our story is that Robert and I are two hikers who got off the trail and got lost in the woods. Totally innocent."

"Thank god you found me," Judy whispers. "They've got me locked in here. I think they're going to kill me."

"We're going to get you out. We can't do it right now, but we'll be back for you soon."

"You'd better act like you never saw me. If they find out you did, they're not going to let you go. I could be killed at any moment, so hurry."

"Help is coming," Robert says as they back away from the window and head across the clearing toward the barn.

"What is that smell?" Robert asks.

"It's pretty foul."

"I think it's fertilizer."

"Well this is a farm," Marie points out.

"Not like any farm you'll ever see. I don't see anything that needs fertilizing."

Houses and buildings are tucked in the woods at the edge of the clearing, all served by a large loop driveway, and all facing a tall flagpole and central lawn. The pole flies two flags, a large red and black Swastika and also a white cross on a field of red. Robert nods toward security cameras at several points around the clearing, including one on what appears to be a chapel.

"Are those bunkers?" Robert asks, pointing toward several

earthen mounds with heavy plank doors.

"Yeah," Marie agrees. "Or caves. Beyond them, it looks like there's a firing range with silhouettes of men suspended from trolley wires. Is that even legal?"

"I think so. Shane told me that in Island County, property owners are allowed to have firing ranges on private land."

"So what's in the caves? Munitions? This is like a military post," Marie remarks.

"No idea. This is all new to me."

At the barn, they start around the side.

"Hold it right there," a man's voice calls from behind. "That's far enough. Didn't you see the signs?"

"What signs?" Marie replies, turning to face a crewcut man in a paramilitary uniform, his hand on the holster of a sidearm.

"This is a private, religious community totally closed to the public. Trespassing is expressly forbidden."

"Boy are we glad to see you," Marie replies, disregarding the man's menacing tone. "Are we close to the Wilbert Trail? We are completely lost."

"That is god's truth," Robert adds, "and it's entirely my fault."

The man pulls a microphone from a walkie-talkie strapped to his body and speaks into it. "I've got two bogeys in custody by the barn."

A burst of static and some incomprehensible words come back over the radio.

"I think you're poking around where you don't belong," the man says.

"I am sorry if we're in the wrong place," Robert replies, "but my god I nearly killed my wife dragging her through the woods. We were hiking on the park trails and I thought we could cut through the woods and get back faster. We need help and some water. My wife's shins are all banged and cut from climbing over fallen trees and wading in the swamp."

No reply.

"Can you point us back to the state park?" Marie asks.

The man studies them.

"Who the hell are you?" he asks with a cynical edge in his voice.

"Robert Yuka from Fairbanks, Alaska, and my wife, Marie,"

Robert says, smiling and holding out his right hand to introduce himself. "We're camping at the park."

The man keeps his right hand on the holster and Robert awkwardly puts his down.

"Let me see some I.D."

Robert reaches into the back pocket of his shorts and brings out his wallet, from which he produces his old Alaska driver's license. He hands it to the man, who studies it.

"Come with me," the man commands. "I think we'd better go talk with somebody."

He leads them across the compound to an old rambler-style farmhouse, where he knocks and a white-haired man in a neatly-pressed, brown shirt answers the door, accompanied by a second guard. Martin recognizes Buford Boh Buckley from the supremacist demonstration a few days ago.

"These are the snoopers I picked up," the guard announces.

"Do I know you?" Buford Boh asks. "I feel like we've met before."

Robert feels a chill. "I don't think so." He hopes Buckley doesn't recognize him as a face in the crowd at the park.

Buckley listens to their explanation, then replies, "Who do you work for? Your story doesn't add up. The woods between the park and here are so dense, I don't believe you could hike through them. There's no trail."

"Believe me," Robert says, "it wasn't something we set out to do. Look at my wife. We still don't know where we are. We're sorry about trespassing on your land but we just want to get back to the park."

"Do you know whose place this is?" Buford Boh asks.

"Some kind of church, according to this man," Robert replies with a nod toward the guard.

"We take our Constitutional freedoms and Second Amendment rights seriously. Certain people would like to get in here and snoop around," Buford Boh continues. "We don't allow that."

Robert thinks it's ironic that the same people who quote the Constitution and Second Amendment for their rights also want to overthrow the government that guarantees those freedoms.

"We completely understand," Marie interjects. "None of this was our idea. When we get back to the park I'm going to kill my husband. We need to get back to our baby. We told our friends who are watching him we'd only be gone a little while when we left on this hike."

"Is that right?" Buford Boh says.

"Yes it is," Robert remarks.

Buford Boh cocks his head pensively and turns toward Robert. "I thought Indians didn't get lost in the woods."

"I'm an Inuit – Alaska native. I'm better with snow and ice. I totally screwed up."

"I would have to agree," Buford Boh remarks. He turns back toward Marie. "We are a white Christian church. We like to see white women marry their own kind. Fewer problems all around."

He beckons one of the guards to come with him as he walks out of the room and leaves Robert and Marie with the other guard.

Marie leans close to Robert's ear. "I didn't think they'd be this long letting us go."

"It makes you wonder what's the holdup, doesn't it?" Robert replies.

He looks out the window and sees Fred Franks and Raymond Cobb leave the barn and walk toward the house.

"Oh oh."

*

Brad stands behind Shane in his study and watches a blinking display on Shane's computer.

The display marks the GPS transmitter's location on a Google Earth view of the woods by the Buckley compound. The blinking light hasn't moved in an hour but tells him two things – that Robert and Marie made it to the unfenced back boundary of the compound, and that Marie probably jettisoned the transmitter as they agreed in advance, so Buckley's men wouldn't discover they were carrying it.

At this point there is nothing further to learn until Robert and Marie emerge from this place where, no doubt, they are most unwelcome. If security is lax, they may be able to look around before they are captured. If not, they are already trying to talk their way out – two bumbling fools who blundered into the wrong place.

"The Buckleys won't be happy about outsiders in the compound," Shane points out, "but what can they do, really, but let them go?"

"You hope."

"Right. I hope. The thing that could really mess this up is if they get caught looking at something they shouldn't. I told them to be super careful and play dumb if that happens."

"Doesn't it make you nervous that you've sent them in there without a search warrant? Can you use any of this in court?"

"Yes to your first question. No to the second. But if Judy's in danger we need to get her out, and we just don't have any basis to go in there on police grounds."

Shane's cell phone rings. He reaches for it eagerly, then scowls when he sees the caller display.

"Is it them?" Brad asks.

"No, it's one of our conservative county commissioners, Bill Biggs."

"Shane Lindstrom," he answers, and then listens.

"I understand, he says."

Long pause.

"I understand your position on this, Bill."

Long pause.

"My concern is that we have a missing woman and it's increasingly likely her disappearance is linked to Jerry Buckley."

Pause.

"No I can't prove that. And yes it's my ex-wife. You understand I didn't initiate this situation. It's something Judy did on her own."

Pause.

"You're right we don't have any specific evidence of foul play. I know we have to tread carefully."

Pause.

"I will, commissioner," Shane says, and pushes *end*.

He rolls his eyes. "What a mess."

Elizabeth and Irene enter the room. Irene holds baby Martin across her shoulder, and she's patting his back. "What's going on?" she asks.

"He wants me to back off the Buckleys."

"Seriously?" Elizabeth asks.

"He says it smacks of harassment and persecution of a religious organization. What he didn't say is that the Buckleys are a long-time island family and staunch contributors to his campaign."

"Religious?" Brad asks. "He must have meant racist."

"I'm sure he meant what he said. The county relies on a lot of federal grants and he doesn't want anything jeopardizing them."

"Isn't it rather unusual for an elected official to call a sheriff's deputy directly on his private line about something like this, instead of going through the sheriff?"

"I think he wanted to be sure I got the message clearly."

"Is your job on the line?" Elizabeth asks.

"It always is," Shane replies.

*

"Well here's some comic relief for you," Irene says as she gets out her sketchpad and pens. "The president wants a military parade."

"A what?" Brad asks.

"A big military parade with tanks and troops and missiles in the streets," Irene adds. "And fly-overs. It was just on TV, the announcement."

"Cool," Billy says.

"Like Mussolini and Hitler and Kim Jong-un?" Brad asks.

"Yeah, like that."

"Dear lord. By the way, what are you going to sketch?"

"I'm not sure," she replies, looking around. "Maybe some still lifes of the décor. There are so many antiques in this room."

"Shane and Elizabeth might enjoy having a few sketches."

"Tell me you were just pulling my leg about the military parade."

"You'd like to think so, wouldn't you? The president says he sees it as a day of national unity," she continues, "so he's opening it up to veterans carrying Confederate flags and to the Ku Klux Klan, and any other supremacist and paramilitary groups to join in."

"Well nothing will unify the country like a divisive parade," Brad says with a smirk. "Luckily, he keeps pointing out he's the least-racist person anyone ever met."

As they talk, Billy studies with a magnifying glass several of the rocks that Bolivar sent, looking them up in a book about minerals from the library.

"I have an idea," Irene announces, looking at Billy. "Would

you like me to make a sketch of you looking at those rocks that we can send to Bolivar?"

"Yes," Billy replies. "I'll bet he would like that."

"Keep looking with that magnifying glass," Irene says. She studies the scene for a moment, then begins to draw on the pad. Shane walks in with a cup of coffee and pauses behind Irene to look over her shoulder.

"I like it," he says. "I'd like a copy of that when you're done."

"Let's see if you still feel that way in a little while."

"Dad?" Billy asks.

"Yes."

"Mom hasn't called for several days. I want to tell her about the rocks Bolivar sent me."

"Have you tried calling her?"

"I just get voice mail."

"Well, keep trying," Shane replies nonchalantly. "That's all you can do. She must be busy with something."

Chapter 13

When Buford Boh Buckley re-enters the room, Robert instantly notices his expression has darkened.

"It seems we have an awkward situation," Buford Boh declares, forcing a smile. "One of my associates tells me he remembers you from the memorial service the other day at the park."

"I didn't want to make an issue of it," Robert begins, "but that's right; I was there. It was a total coincidence."

"Well then maybe you'd better enlighten me."

"Marie and I are camping at the park. I already explained that. When I saw all the police and protesters I wondered what was happening. It was quite a spectacle so I grabbed my camera and went over there and shot some video. That event was a lot more exciting than anything else we've seen so far on this vacation."

Buford Boh slams his fist on the table. Marie winces and Robert puts his arm around her.

"How gullible do you think we are, Mr. Yuka? I think your whole story is lies. You film us at the park and then you come blundering through the woods and accidentally find yourselves on private property. What a coincidence."

Robert and Marie stand silently.

"Take their pictures, please, Brett," Buford Boh says to the guard, who pulls out a cell phone and snaps several images. "I like to have evidence. I'll tell you this," Buford Boh continues. "I have a pretty good idea who you are working for and I'm taking this to the county. The commissioners do not take this heavy-handed harassment of private citizens lightly."

Buford Boh turns to the guard. "Get them out of here."

The guard escorts them to the main gate, pushes a button on his walkie talkie and the gate swings open. He points to the right. "Down the road a few miles."

The gate swings shut and the guard turns away and heads up the driveway toward the compound. Robert and Marie start to walk.

"What a creep," Marie remarks.

Robert smiles.

The early evening sun is low in the sky, throwing long shadows from the taller trees.

Moments later, they flag down a car and borrow the driver's cell phone.

"We're out," Robert tells Shane. "Judy is being held there, unable to leave, and we talked to her through a small window in the cabin where you thought she was. Franks and Cobb came out of the barn later and walked over to the house. Cobb recognized me from the park, which blew what little credibility our story had. Buford Boh didn't buy anything we said. Judy says her life is in danger."

He hangs up and looks at Marie. "Brad is on the way to pick us up. Shane is working on a search warrant."

*

Judy paces back and forth in the tiny cabin. It's just growing dark when she hears a car approach on the loop drive and stop outside. She quickly sits down on the bed. The car door clicks open and then slams shut with a thunk. Keys jingle in the cabin lock again and Jerry comes in, breathing hard. "Get up," he announces. "We're getting out of here right now."

"What's going on?"

"Change of plans. I'm sorry, but I have to do this," he says. He takes her by the shoulders and turns her around, zip-ties her hands behind her back, then leads her out the door. On the far side of the compound, she notices the barn doors opening and two men walking out. The violent guy, Ray, looks right at her. He watches Jerry put Judy into his car.

Then Ray gets into the box truck with his partner and they drive out. Brown-shirted guards stand around, tense and alert, their hands resting on pistols in holsters.

Judy wonders if this is the big moment at last. Is this the end for her? Jerry sits at the wheel for a moment, looking across the seat at her, then reaches across and buckles her seatbelt.

He starts the car, drives to the gate, opens it and heads for the highway, where he turns toward the Clinton ferry terminal. Judy tries to pay attention to where they are going. If she gets a chance to make a break for it, she's going to need to know where she is. It all seems moot anyway. Realistically, what chance does she have with her hands tied behind her back?

At a highway shopping center part way to the ferry, Jerry turns south. This is the way to Possession Point, one of the most remote areas of the island. The roads get narrower and narrower, and the forest grows closer around them. It is dark now and the headlights illuminate a cone of pavement and trees. After some time, he slows and turns up a narrow, gravel drive pitted with deep chuckholes. He drives slowly, weaving right and left to avoid the worst holes. Half a mile later they emerge in a clearing with a small cabin. Jerry shuts off the headlights and it is totally dark.

They sit in the car for a moment. Judy senses he is thinking, perhaps studying the cabin before walking up to it. Or maybe he is working up the courage to kill her in this remote place. A body could go undiscovered here for a very long time – till it's just dry bones in a shallow grave, scattered by coyotes.

"This is it," he announces at last.

"This is *what*?" Judy replies.

"Home for tonight."

With a flashlight, Jerry guides her to the cabin door and unlocks it. Inside, in the mudroom, Judy is surprised to see a moped. The kitchen is well stocked with basics – oatmeal, canned meat and vegetables, dried fruit, a tin of coffee and even some chocolate bars.

She feels a wave of relief. She's still alive. She will make this night worth his while. It may not be much, but sex is the only tool she has right now unless there's a knife in one of the drawers.

"Let's go make ourselves at home," Judy says, "and I'll see if I can make this a night to remember for you."

"I don't know why you're so good to me. I treat you like dirt."

"You know what they say," singing 'When you're born a woman, you're born to be dirt.' "But dang me, just the sight of you makes me horny."

*

At Shane's office in Coupeville, he races against time to assemble the team and equipment he needs for a raid on the compound. The judge signs his search warrant. He is good to go.

At 10 p.m. Shane calls the Rev. Buford Boh Buckley from a darkened police helicopter hovering over a field a quarter of a mile away. "I have a search warrant and my helicopter will set down in your compound in less than a minute," he says. "Other officers are at the gate right now. Please open the gate immediately or they will destroy it. I expect your full cooperation."

The helicopter ascends two hundred feet, switches on its landing lights and a blinding search light, and accelerates forward at treetop level to the compound. It sweeps its searchlight across half-a-dozen of Buckley's brown-shirted men, staring up at the sky in a semi-circle on the edge of the clearing, their sidearms all still holstered. The chopper descends in a cloud of dust and blowing debris. As its turbine spools down, four officers in tactical gear, led by Shane, jump out and run straight for Judy's cabin. Twenty more in the uniforms of various jurisdictions come up the road from the gate. An officer from the helicopter approaches Buford Boh with a copy of the warrant.

Shane looks back at the main house and sees Buford Boh in the open doorway, his jaw hanging open as the officer hands him the warrant. Shane can't hear Buford Boh's response but imagines it is something along the lines of an outrageous and massive violation of his Constitutional rights. Shane silently prays they'll find Judy. Billy needs his mom. And Shane is risking the last of his credibility on this search.

When he tries the door to Judy's cabin he finds it unlocked. The tiny room is empty and the bed is unmade. A carafe of coffee, still warm, sits on the burner. He turns to the deputy behind him and instructs, "Get somebody in here with a fingerprint kit, and search all the other buildings." He rushes out.

Other deputies fan out across the compound. "Search everything thoroughly," he instructs them. "They've moved her and she may still be on the premises. There may be caves or tunnels. Look for trap doors."

A dozen officers in sheriff's cruisers come up the road from the main gate. The cars stop in the central clearing. Officers emerge in tactical gear and begin working their way from building to building. Shane heads directly for the barn. The odor of fertilizer is heavy in the atmosphere but the barn is empty. A fire smolders in a burn barrel but he finds nothing but empty sacks, smoldering.

"Let's take our time and be thorough," Shane declares. But his hopes already are sinking. Buford Boh walks toward him across the compound, indignant, followed by several of his somber-faced security detail.

"Finding what you're looking for?" he asks with a bitter tone.

"I'll let you know when we're done. I'm going to have a lot of questions for you."

Shane walks to the nearest bunker, pulls open the heavy door and steps inside with another officer. It smells like a dusty garage – a mixture of fresh concrete and musty earth. He runs his flashlight along the walls and is surprised at how well the underground unit is built and stocked. The walls are finished and are lined with cedar plank shelves holding crates of ammunition, gas masks and rifles and shotguns. A dozen AR-15 assault rifles are stored in a locked rack.

There is also canned food – peaches, stew, spam and vegetables – large bags of rice, foil packets of freeze-dried meals, and dozens of five-gallon jugs of water and gasoline. He takes stock of assorted knives and axes, walkie-talkies, flashlights and batteries, a hand-crank radio, oil lamps, duct tape, waterproof matches, pepper spray, mylar blankets, pain pills and first aid supplies. There is no hint Judy was ever here.

He looks for shelving that rotates to provide access to another chamber but finds nothing, and instructs the other officer to keep looking while he steps outside.

Buford Boh is waiting outside when Shane emerges. "The guns are all legal," Buford Boh remarks.

"There must be several dozen jugs of bleach," a deputy remarks. "What's with that?"

"Water purification," Buford Boh remarks.

"What's with the lye?" Shane asks, pointing toward a large tub.

"Multiple uses."

Shane looks right at the preacher. "I have two witnesses who saw a woman in that cabin a few hours ago," he says, pointing across the compound. "She told them she was being held against her will.

What can you tell me about that?"

Shane senses this catches Buford Boh by surprise. "Nothing," he replies. "By witnesses I assume you mean that flakey Alaska couple who trespassed on my property. By the way that was an illegal search initiated by you, so you can be sure I'm reporting it to your bosses. I don't know what those people think they saw, but it wasn't any prisoner."

"So you don't even know if a woman was staying in that cabin?"

"The cabin belongs to my son and he isn't here," Buford Boh says. "Sometimes his girlfriend visits."

"Well I hope you'll get a message to him that he needs to contact us immediately. As of right now he is a person of interest in a kidnapping. And if you shelter him, you are an accessory.

"Another thing," Shane continues. "There is a strong odor of nitrate in your barn," Shane says.

"We've been known to use fertilizer," Buford Boh replies. "We grow a lot of our own food here."

"You've had some people staying with you," Shane goes on, "Fred Franks and Raymond Cobb. I'd like to talk with them."

"They came out to the island for the memorial at the state park and stayed here for a few days."

"Where might I find them?"

"Honestly, I don't know," Buford Boh says. "I believe they have already left."

"Just in the last few hours?"

"I believe so."

Shane reaches for the microphone on his chest. He requests surveillance tonight of both ferry crossings and Deception Pass Bridge for a Budget box truck with two men and a load of ammonium nitrate fertilizer, and for a car carrying Jerry and Judy. But in his heart he fears it is already too late to stop Cobb and Franks. He hopes to get lucky but knows too many hours have passed. He has already lost the element of surprise.

*

The mood in the Suburban is heavy as Shane pulls into the lot by the Maxwelton Beach baseball field and the group gets out. A handful of kids and dads play ball at the diamond. The early-evening sun bathes the beach in golden tones.

It's been a long and depressing day after the previous night's unsuccessful raid. Shane's been on the phone to his office for hours. He and Robert have huddled for hours more, going over what happened.

Marie suggests this evening walk on the beach so they can get out of the house and clear their heads. The scene here is reassuringly normal. Getaway cabins and homes line the sandy shoreline. Part way down the beach, a solitary young girl throws a driftwood stick for a Golden Retriever. The dog splashes into the surf and swims out, gets the stick in its mouth and paddles back to shore. When its paws touch the bottom it races back to the girl and drops the stick at her feet, then shakes itself vigorously from side to side in a cloud of cold spray. The girl turns away, cringes and squeals.

"Ah, to be that girl again," Marie says as she watches. "Just a carefree girl and her dog on a summer evening at the beach."

"Right now I wouldn't mind being that girl, either," Shane says. "I'm supposed to be off work these two weeks but I triggered a raid that apparently spooked the bad guys and my boss is furious."

It's clear Shane needs to de-stress, Marie thinks, and go over what they know about the Buckley situation and discuss strategy. They left Irene and Elizabeth back at the inn to watch Billy and Martin. Irene jumps at the chance to give Elizabeth and Billy some sketching lessons in the shady front yard.

"This is a cute community," Marie declares, feeling like an airhead for saying it on such a charged day. But she knows Shane likes to talk about the island, this place he loves.

"There's a lot of history here at Maxwelton Beach," Shane says. "This is the outlet of the largest watershed on the island, and the only stream with a salmon run. The early settlers diked and altered it for farming and flood control. But when they got here you could actually sail a small boat inland a little at high tide. Remnants of an old Spanish vessel were found in the mud."

"Well that's cool," Martin notes.

"And in 1910 the Chautauqua was held right here. That was about when Freeland was settled and the brothel got its start. People traveled by ship from all over Puget Sound to camp and hold meetings here at Maxwelton, and hear speakers. They even had the famous evangelist, Billy Sunday, and a ladies' orchestra."

The group walks on, soaking up the onshore breeze and the sweet, smoky aroma of the occasional beach fire. Brad thinks about all the changes this island has seen from Spanish explorers to farmers to socialists, cultural reformers and evangelists, and now, it seems, separatists who feel threatened by Muslims and Latinos, and people from "shithole countries," as the president puts it.

"So where do we stand?" Brad asks.

"The raid got us nothing," Shane replies. "Except that I'm hanging by a thread with my boss."

"Actually I think you got a lot," Robert remarks. "We absolutely know that Judy was in that compound and was being held captive. That is a fact because Marie and I talked with her. We know Cobb and Franks were there because you filmed them coming and going on several occasions," Robert adds.

"Somebody rented a box truck on the mainland and bought ammonium nitrate fertilizer from several farm stores," Brad says.

". . . which we did not find, but the smell of which was heavy in the air at the Buckley compound," Shane points out.

"And all of them cleared out as soon as Buford Boh released Marie and me," Robert adds.

"Which means something was going on there that was so important none of them could afford to be there when you showed up," Brad interjects. "It was just your bad luck, Shane, that by the time you got in there with the search warrant, they had cleaned up and moved on."

*

Lying in the hay with his eyes closed, Fred Franks is pretty sure sheriff's deputies and state patrol officers are reviewing footage right now from dozens of ferry cams and highway traffic cams throughout the Puget Sound corridor. They are slogging through thousands of hours of video, a tedious and thankless job. By now they have isolated hundreds of box trucks on film but only a handful that are Budget rentals of the right length, and none with the license number of the one parked in the barn beside him, since he switched the plates.

It's pitch black when he hears the rooster crow. Dear god!

Rolling over and checking the luminous dial of his wristwatch, he sees it is 4 a.m. He hears something scratch at the hay in the darkness. It's either a chicken or a rat. He hates this. He supposes this barn has bats, also.

It's all coming back to him now, knowledge he gained when he worked as an exterminator for a few months.

Deer mice can spread Hantavirus, a pulmonary virus fatal to humans. They do it in dusty places like this where particles of dried feces get disturbed and become airborne. He won't tell Ray this. Ray is angry and impatient enough, hard enough to keep on task.

On the other hand, maybe the rats are really their friends. He's pretty sure rats and mice won't live together in the same space. So if this barn is full of rats, maybe it doesn't have mice.

The barn is just four miles from the Buckley compound, half a mile up a gravel lane that ends at a pasture in the woods. The chickens enter and leave through a small hole five feet up on the siding – too small for coyotes. An automatic feeder with a timer dispenses grain for the flock twice a day. Two cows graze in the fenced pasture. It's an ingenious safe house, he thinks – good work on Jerry's part.

It took about ten minutes to drive here the other night. Now they wait.

Franks assures Cobb this is a smart move – lying low. The game now is to sit tight and let the search go cold. He hopes Jerry got away clean, too, because he is their meals on wheels.

In the distance Franks hears the soft purr of a moped coming up the gravel. That would be Jerry. They've agreed on no cell phone contact unless it's urgent because phones can be traced.

Franks turns on a battery-powered lantern, gets up and walks to the door, opens it a crack and watches a cone of light from the moped's headlamp come up the road. Jerry stops out front and kills the engine, grabs a backpack from his cycle and joins Franks in the barn. Cobb is stirring now.

"Any trouble last night?" Franks asks Jerry.

"Not a bit. Made it to the safe house in good shape."

"And the girl?"

"I put her in the ground."

*

Brad is up early in the darkness, dressed and thinking about coffee. After the night sweat, he can't get back to sleep. Irene is sleeping soundly and he can't hear a soul stirring in the house, but when he opens the door and heads toward the kitchen, the light up ahead is already on. Elizabeth stands over the coffeemaker as it gurgles, willing it to finish and shut itself off. She turns and faces Brad when she discovers she's not alone.

"Up to your old tricks, I see," Elizabeth greets him.

"You, too."

"I'm a morning person."

"I know."

"This fresh pot has our names on it," she says, taking two cups off their hooks and filling one for each of them. They pull out chairs from the table and sit down.

"Nice to have some quiet time for us to visit," Elizabeth says, "just the two of us, like old times."

"You must feel like a widow right now with Shane so preoccupied."

"Yeah, it's a bit like that sometimes," she agrees. "But it comes and goes with the job."

Brad takes a sip of his coffee and puts down the cup.

"So tell me honestly," he begins, "does it feel a little close at times, having Judy so nearby?"

Elizabeth smiles. "Well, if you're asking for honesty, I will say she generates some extra drama in our lives. Like this thing right now. We go from one crisis to the next and she always seems to pull Shane in."

Brad nods. "It can't go on forever. He's in a real predicament. If something happens to Judy it's going to devastate Billy."

"Plus," Elizabeth adds, "his boss isn't too happy with him right now. The county commissioners think he's harassing the Buckleys. He already lost his job once in Island County over the Bella investigation. He got it back and we bought this place, and things were going well. But now this."

"Are you worried?" Brad asks. "How are you doing?"

"Well if you lay Judy aside, I've never been as happy as I am right now, right here."

"That's a good way to look at it."

They sit a moment while Brad tries to read between the lines of that answer. Then Elizabeth looks up and asks, "But I haven't really asked about you. How have you been since we saw you last year in Idaho?"

"Oh, you know, not bad but not getting any younger. Things pile up on you in your seventies. I guess I'm feeling my age."

She studies him closely. "I wondered. I don't see the usual energy and spirit. I wondered if you might be a little run down."

"Not sleeping my best these days," he admits. "It's an age thing."

"Have you seen a doctor lately?" she asks.

*

Ida Mae Buckley pulls four sweet pickles from the jar with tongs. She dices them into fine bits and pushes them to the side of the cutting board, then goes back to the refrigerator for four stalks of celery and half a red onion, and repeats the same process.

When all three items have been diced, she scoops them into a large mixing bowl and opens the first of two oversize cans of tuna, and a jar of mayonnaise. She sets the tuna liquid aside in a small bowl as two cats appear from nowhere and throw themselves at her feet, rolling upside down, bellowing and staring at the counter.

She divides the liquid into a second bowl and sets both dishes on the floor. The cats jump to their feet and begin slurping loudly.

Ida Mae adds a generous dollop of mayonnaise to the large bowl and mashes the mixture with a fork till she's satisfied with the consistency. She takes a small taste from the fork and adds more mayo.

Then she lays out eight slices of white bread on the counter and slathers four of them generously with the tuna. She covers those four with the remaining four slices, cuts the sandwiches diagonally and inserts them into baggies.

She carefully positions all four in the bottom of a backpack, next to several cartons of juice and chocolate milk, and a pack of blue ice. A thermos of coffee slides into a side pocket. She tops the backpack with a freezer bag of two dozen chocolate chip cookies, adds some napkins and paper cups, zips the whole thing shut and places it on the kitchen table.

"Ready!" she yells.

Buford Boh appears from the next room, takes the backpack and heads out the door. He gets into his old Chevy pickup and drives to the gate, takes a left and drives exactly four miles to a 35 mph sign, where he pulls onto the shoulder. He gets out, grabs the backpack off the front seat and walks ten feet into the brush where he sets the backpack behind a bush. Then he returns to the truck and drives home.

*

"What is it?" Raymond Cobb asks as Jerry sets down the backpack. Ray has been cleaning and oiling his grenade launcher but sets it down when Jerry appears, and wipes his hands on an old T-shirt.

Fred Franks unzips the pack and pulls out a bag of home-baked cookies.

"Chocolate chip," Franks says, pulling the big bag of cookies off the top.

"The mother lode!"

"Those aren't all for you," Jerry cautions. "I'm taking some with me."

Franks digs deeper, pulls out a sandwich and sniffs it. "Tuna."

"Seriously? What else is in there?" Cobb asks.

"That's all," Jerry replies. "She loves tuna."

"That's repulsive," Cobb says.

Franks forages some more and comes up with chocolate milk. "This will go down easy."

The three men sit down to their picnic in the hay.

"There'd better be some beer in the next delivery," Ray says.

When they're done, Jerry gathers up the backpack and several of the cookies, and the extra tuna sandwich, and heads for his bike.

"I'll be back later with dinner . . . and some beers."

Franks yells after him, "Turkey next time. Or ham. Okay?"

*

Brad finds Shane in his office, staring vacantly at a Google

Earth view of the island on his computer screen. The large patches of forest that normally make it so beautiful also make it impenetrable.

"Anything?" Brad asks.

"Absolutely nothing," Shane declares, throwing his hands in the air. "They've disappeared into thin air. I don't know if they all got off the island or if they went underground to another safe house. No one has seen the truck anywhere. Nor have we seen Jerry."

"So presumably the three of them are together."

"Presumably, but where does that leave Judy?" Shane wonders aloud. "Is she with them or against them? Dead or alive?"

"What's happening at the compound?" Brad asks. "Is it possible Judy was there the whole time but you didn't find her?"

"Anything is possible," Shane says. "We're still watching the compound but it's dead quiet. It's like we just imagined the whole thing with Cobb and Franks."

*

At the clearing's edge, where the tall grass and brush give way to trees, Cobb begins to dig. It's a remote spot some distance from an isolated building at the end of a private, forest lane nobody uses. Sweat runs down Cobb's forehead from his bald head and stings his eyes. From his back pocket he extracts a red bandanna and ties it across his forehead.

Cobb digs three large sword ferns with generous root balls and sets them aside on a tarp with the rest of the dirt from the hole. Now the work becomes harder. The earth here is a few inches of soft organic material on top of rocky cobble packed hard by the weight of a mile-deep glacier, thousands of years ago.

With an axe he cuts through a shallow web of tree roots on which the ferns grow. He chops the woody roots into bits and pieces, and throws them deep into the nearby woods, where dense salal and huckleberry brush swallows them.

A feeling grows inside him that he's not alone. Heart pounding, he stops, straightens up and looks around for something that does not belong. He scans the trees and shadows, and suddenly registers two large, yellow eyes and sharp-pointed ears staring right at him.

It's a Great-horned Owl thirty feet away in a fir tree, backlit in the shadows. The owl follows every move; its eyes unnerve him, seeming to know too much.

The two beings study each other across the species barrier, neither breaking his gaze. Then finally, Cobb turns his back and returns to his work. With a pick he breaks loose a little of the cobble and scoops it out of the hole with his shovel, then goes back to the pick. He feels those eyes watching the back of his head.

He makes the hole four feet long and three feet wide. That part is easy, but he wants it four feet deep and it's slow work. His dad beat the lesson into him with a belt – dig your holes tidy and straight. At four feet there won't be much odor for a dog to sniff, no bones to scatter, not that a dog ever comes this way.

When he's satisfied with the hole, he puts the shovel aside and reaches into his shirt pocket for a cigarette. He lights it and takes a few puffs. When he looks up again at the trees, the owl is gone.

Chapter 14

The body is on its side, in the fetal position. The wound on the forehead is gruesome, deep and ugly. It bled profusely and leaked some gray ooze onto the ground. Cobb removes identification and personal effects, spreads a blue tarp and lifts the stiff corpse awkwardly onto it, then grabs two corners of the tarp and starts to pull. It slides easily, confined to the tarp, leaving no blood trail, across the clearing to the forest edge.

At the hole he drags the body and tarp right into it. The body lands in the bottom face up, legs up, staring at him with open eyes, in that classic expression of surprise. The last thing those eyes saw when they awoke was him holding a cinder block high overhead.

In a longer hole, the body would lie flat but he dug this one deep enough it doesn't matter.

He wads the rest of the tarp into the hole and refills it, starting with the head, throwing dirt into the corpse's face. Rocks and sand, little by little, erase those eyes.

He fills the hole all the way, smoothes and lightly packs the mound with his boots, and then digs three shallow depressions and replants the sword ferns he dug earlier. He spreads a layer of leaves, dry fir needles, rotten branches and forest debris around them on the disturbed earth. When he's done, there is little to catch the eye, just a slight anomaly in the undergrowth. It feels like rain, which will freshen the ferns. Weather and time soon will remove any traces.

He gathers up his tools, hoists them over his shoulder and heads back, whistling a few bars of, "Whistle a Happy Tune," the happiest he's felt in some time.

*

One month earlier. "This is just to help you relax," the nurse says, opening a tap in the intravenous line and injecting something into it. "You're next. We'll be getting started in a few minutes."

Brad's been sitting in this room for hours, separated by curtains on rollers from the patients on either side, a few feet away. From time to time he watches someone wheel by. He's making small talk with Irene, who is sketching the charge nurse, who is a bit roly poly but pleasant. Brad likes her, but Irene says he likes all nurses. Irene is easily bored, which he knows is why she's sketching. It keeps her hands busy.

The nurse keeps glancing Irene's way. Brad supposes the nurse is hoping Irene will show her the sketch. Irene says it isn't finished and isn't very good, and she's self-conscious. She doesn't offer. She's stalling for time, Brad knows, hoping the nurse will get busy and distracted before she can come right out and ask.

Someone comes in with paperwork for him to sign. This is a religiously affiliated medical center and they want to know his faith preference. He writes atheist.

"Really?" she asks.

Brad doesn't answer.

A simple thing like this procedure blows the whole day, Brad reflects, and there's too much time to think. Relax isn't the right word for this. But on the other hand, he doesn't much care what they do to him.

Moments later, two assistants roll a gurney into the room and position it alongside Brad's bed. One of them folds a warm blanket over Brad's legs and then, with his help, they slide him from the bed onto the gurney.

Irene blows him a kiss from her chair in the corner. "See you in a few minutes," she says as they wheel him out. It's a quick ride past several other bored patients, through double swinging doors into a cold hallway and then through another set of double doors into what looks like an industrial, stainless-steel kitchen, or possibly a slaughterhouse, where several women in blue scrubs are dancing.

Rock music blares from speakers in the ceiling.

"Turn that down a little, will you?" asks the woman who appears to be in charge. The volume drops. She leans over Brad's face so he can see her clearly and says, "It lightens the mood around here. Any requests? Led Zeppelin?"

Brad shakes his head. He isn't much of a rock fan.

"Jesus Loves Me?" she asks.

Brad winces. Is this a joke? Did she read the paperwork he just signed? This procedure isn't supposed to be fatal, is it? They like the word "procedure."

The woman continues, "When we get going, we'll give you a little pulse of anesthesia in the I.V. line and you shouldn't feel anything. If you need more, raise your hand. I just need to do some measuring and mark a few spots on your neck and collar to be sure we're in the right place."

Brad wonders how often they dig into the wrong place.

She pokes and prods, and draws some lines with a black marker.

"Ready?" she asks. "Any last words?"

"No."

*

"Finished," Brad hears through the haze. Rock music blares again from the speakers and three women lean over him.

"Have you started yet?" Brad asks.

"You're finished," one of them says. "Looks like we got a nice bunch of cells," and the gurney starts to move again.

*

Brad wonders how many months or years he carried this inside him. He'd been tired for months, going to bed early, slightly "off." Awareness came slowly, with a cold last December that didn't want to end. Then the sweats began and turned into what he assumed was walking pneumonia. He saw his doctor and she ordered labs.

"This doesn't look right," she said when she got the numbers. "You need to get this checked out. I'm referring you to Boise."

A week later he sat in a big recliner in a tiny exam room in Boise and waited for the woman he nicknamed for the state capital. The clop clop of hard heels in the hallway alerted him that a busy woman with a purpose approached. There was a suspenseful pause, a light tap on the door, and then it swung open.

Dr. Chu Hua turned out to be a Chinese hematologist and oncologist, a young woman with a pretty face and soft eyes, a warm smile and a file in her hand. Her name means Chrysanthemum – he already knows this from the Internet. He also knows from her online biography that she's the only daughter of a mom who lives in a small town in rural China and was a nurse in the Cultural Revolution. He supposes Boise is a product of the one-child policy. A daughter would be a disappointment, he suspects. She did her medical school at a university he never heard of in Mainland China, followed by two years at Fred Hutchinson in Seattle. He hopes the Chinese university was a good one. He hopes Boise has some friends at Fred Hutch.

How times have changed since Nixon opened China to the West.

"Good morning, Bradford," she says, shaking his hand properly. "How do you feel today?" She looks into his eyes. Do they teach eye contact in medical school? Norwegians avoid it, but he doesn't mind it from her. He just feels like he can't hide anything from her.

She seems genuinely interested, so he tells her – a bit tired, rundown, feverish. He expected she'd be more of a nerd but doesn't say that. She appears smart. He likes this confident woman with the interesting English and easy sense of humor. But between the laughs and her reassurance that they're going to figure this out, she loses no time looking deeper.

"I'd like to do a little exam," she says, slipping on latex gloves. Just untuck your shirt and lie back in the chair. She pokes and pushes at his abdomen, exploring his organs, his neck and his armpits. "Unremarkable," she says, slipping off the gloves.

That's what they all say, Brad thinks.

"Would you be willing to have a bone marrow biopsy?" she asks. "I'd like to see what's happening in the marrow, where your blood cells form." He's heard stories about this – a special kind of pain – so when she says he can have it with or without anesthesia, he chooses "with."

The result is encouraging beyond anything he dares hope. "Your biopsy was unremarkable," she says.

This word, "unremarkable," he's since learned, is a favorite of doctors like Boise. It doesn't mean you're sick or well, just that they didn't find anything.

"So," Brad asks her, "this means I don't have cancer?"

"Not necessarily," she says. "Sometimes the cancer cells hide in pockets. There's something else we could do if you're willing."

"Absolutely," Brad says.

So she orders a full body CT scan – a slow ride on a flatbed trolley through what looks like a big metal doughnut that takes three-dimensional X-rays.

Bingo.

"Your lymph nodes are way too large," she says. "It is suggestive of lymphoma."

"How bad is it?" Brad asks.

"I don't know. I still need to see some cells. The easiest place to get them probably is this enlarged gland in your neck," she says, pointing to the picture in his file.

*

The meeting with Boise was a month ago. This morning, three states away at a peaceful inn overlooking Holmes Harbor, it all seems surreal to Brad as he tries to leave Boise behind and focus on friends, and on something sinister that seems to be imminent. If only they could put the pieces together.

*

Just a few miles away, the summer sun is climbing over the treetops as Jerry comes up the lane on his moped. The sunrise is red and it feels like the start of a warm day. He passes only a handful of vehicles on the ride over here, and no police or sheriff's cars.

Breakfast in the backpack is scrambled eggs and bacon, which his mom prepares at Jerry's request. He expects this will be a hit with his restless friends. Jerry and his dad have continued the blind relay routine, so that Jerry has gone nowhere near the compound since the night of the raid.

The chickens are out in the yard, scratching at the ground, and all is quiet as he approaches. He stops the bike out front, puts it up on its kickstand and grabs the backpack. The guys don't even get up anymore and come outside to see who it is.

He opens the door and . . . shit!

Shit! Shit! Shit!

Cobb and Franks are gone. The truck is gone. They've changed the plan.

*

Judy needs to pee again and this is a problem because she's handcuffed to the bed. This is Jerry's routine when he rides off for a couple of hours on the moped. He doesn't say where he's going but usually comes back in an hour or two with a sandwich.

Peeing is one thing, but more to the point, she needs to get out of this place while he's gone. She's been over every inch of this cabin. Jerry has cleaned it well of potential weapons and tools. . .

. . . except that her eye notices a paperclip on the floor, just out of reach. She stretches her leg as far as she can, hoping to drag it within reach, but her leg is inches short.

*

After breakfast, Robert and Marie go with Shane to his office in Coupeville, while Irene gives Billy an art lesson in the garden and babysits her favorite new friend, happy-go-lucky Martin.

Brad wanders out to the porch and finds Elizabeth sitting in the sun, reading a trashy novel.

"Pull up a chair," Elizabeth suggests.

"It's a tough life," Brad remarks, taking her suggestion. He watches a butterfly sun itself on a bush, flexing its wings. It's a large and striking insect, orange with black spots, with scalloped wings.

Elizabeth watches him from the corner of her eye.

"Satyr Anglewing," she remarks. "They eat stinging nettles." Suddenly self-conscious, she adds, "Sorry. I can't help myself."

"I think it's delightful you're up to speed on this stuff," Brad remarks.

"I read a lot," she remarks, "and Billy asks lots of questions. Besides, it's good mental health therapy to pay attention to nature." She puts down the novel.

"Speaking of health," she continues, "you didn't really answer my question the other day about the doctor."

"You're going to get it out of me, aren't you?"

"You know I am."

Elizabeth's radar is uncanny, Brad thinks.

"I have Hodgkins Lymphoma."

She stares at him wide-eyed.

"It was pretty far along when it finally got diagnosed," he explains – "after a bad cold, night sweats, blood labs, bone marrow biopsy, CT scan, neck biopsy and some head scratching.

"Treatment hasn't started yet, but will when we get back to Idaho."

He continues, "My oncologist says my platelets are way low and my white cells are way high, so my white cells are trying to fight the cancer but not succeeding. That's why I'm so tired."

Elizabeth says nothing for a moment. "What's the prognosis?"

"Good and bad. The cancer is advanced, which is not good, but it's just in my lymph nodes, which is good. With six months of chemotherapy there's still a pretty good chance I might push it into remission."

He explains he still needs to have surgery to install a port in his chest, on top of his lungs, close to his heart. "That makes me nervous but everyone says it's routine. The drugs are so poisonous they'll fry my veins if I don't have a port by my heart so the chemicals can mix rapidly with the blood after they're infused. That doesn't sound good."

"You need your friends," Elizabeth says. "You need support as you go through this."

"I appreciate that, but right now, I hope we can keep this under wraps. Shane has enough on his plate without my problems distracting him."

*

At Jerry's cabin near Possession Point, Judy studies the paperclip on the floor, just beyond reach of her foot. She is handcuffed by one wrist to the bed. Because of the handcuffs, she can't turn her body around very comfortably to face the wall, but the wall is her only hope at this point.

With pain shooting up her arm to the shoulder joint, she twists her body till one foot reaches the wall. She pushes against it and the bed moves an inch. She does it again, more painfully, and the bed moves some more. Each push is harder and more excruciating than the one before, but each moves the bed precious inches toward the paperclip.

When she is finally satisfied and exhausted, she twists herself the other way till she's lying on her back, one arm extended all the way from the wrist that is handcuffed to the bed and one leg stretched as far as it will go in front of her. It's just barely enough. Her shoe lands on the paperclip and she starts to pull it toward her. A moment later, she holds the paperclip in her hand.

Now for the hard part. Years ago, Shane taught her the trick of picking the lock on a set of handcuffs. She doesn't even remember why – it was just some silly thing they did as a game, and she wanted to learn some of his police tricks.

She unbends the paper clip to get a straight piece of wire, then starts working it back and forth in the cuff, feeling for something to move. It doesn't work at first but she keeps at it till she feels the point of the clip touch a spring-loaded mechanism. She pushes and pulls, and the handcuff pops open.

She's breathing hard and her heart is pounding, but for the first time in days she feels hopeful.

Her wrist hurts and it's red from the contortions she did. She rubs it to regain circulation. Then she stands and crosses the room to the door. The door is locked and she really doesn't think the paperclip will work on a proper lock.

On the porch she finds a double-hung window and opens it, lifts herself up and through it, and falls in a heap into a shrub on the outside. She's ecstatic.

The only problem is that she really doesn't know where she is. She starts to walk, all the while listening for that moped.

*

Elizabeth and Irene stroll a cobblestone path in the lodge's garden, discussing the trees and shrubs. Moss and mint grow between the stones and their shoes release the fragrance of mint as they pass. "You have so much more water here," Irene says. "You can have all this lush landscaping."

"I love the garden in the summertime but we do pay for it in the winter and spring with day-after-day of clouds and rain. That's okay; the winters are cozy for sitting by the fire with a good book, and we both enjoy those hours, too. Winter is our season of rest."

Irene nods as they walk.

"Brad told me about the lymphoma," Elizabeth says, changing the subject.

"Good. Now I don't have to keep the secret any longer. I'm glad he opened up about that. He needs to talk about it."

"How are you handling it?" Elizabeth asks. "Has it pulled the rug out from under your life?"

"To some extent – these things do. Of course, when you get to be seventy you expect surprises. Everyone we know is dealing with something. We all know we can't take anything for granted."

"Are you worried Brad might not make it?"

"Yes and no. Survivability is pretty good with Hodgkin's, but there are no guarantees. He's in stage three, which is pretty far advanced. So he'll have a long course of chemotherapy."

"The what-ifs must weigh on your mind."

Seconds pass before Irene replies.

"They do. If things don't work out for him – for us – I'm not sure I'll stay in Stanley. I may have to give up the ranch and move into the city. Nothing stays the same in life. I don't want to live alone."

"You have Bolivar."

"Yes, with his help I could keep it going, but . . ."

"If you leave, what will become of him?" Elizabeth asks.

"I'd never just walk away from him. I'd make sure he's secure, either to stay with the ranch under a new owner or to get established somewhere else. Bolivar isn't getting any younger, either."

They stop and look out at the waters of Holmes Harbor.

"But it would feel like walking away from your own family," Elizabeth says.

"It would."

"Too many losses all at one time."

Elizabeth turns toward Irene and the two women hug and hold on.

*

Raymond Cobb sits by the truck at a campsite tucked into the trees at Rhododendron Park, near Coupeville on Whidbey Island. He had to leave the hideout and find another place to shelter before Jerry returned. He would rather travel in darkness than daytime, so this campground in the lightly-used county park serves his purpose for a few hours.

There are only a few other campers in the park, some distance away, and he has avoided talking with them. A few of them look semi-permanent, possibly homeless. He chose this spot so he won't be next to anyone.

He sits at a picnic table with the state road map folded open when he notices a county pickup truck coming toward him on the loop road. The truck stops nearby at the restrooms and a middle-aged, black man with a potbelly gets out and walks to the garbage can. He folds back the hinged top and removes a bulging plastic bag from the can, ties it securely and throws it into his truck. Then he replaces it with a new bag.

The county employee looks up and sees Cobb watching him, and he walks over. Cobb assumes that his atypical campsite with the box truck is something the park employees don't see often. This guy must be curious.

"Afternoon," the black man greets him. "Looks like you're doing some trip planning," nodding toward Cobb's map.

"Yeah," Cobb replies. "Throwin' darts at the map." This colored boy is fishing for information, he realizes.

"Which way you going?"

"No idea," Cobb says.

"Will you be here long?" the county employee asks.

Cobb resents having to answer questions for a darkie but can't afford trouble here. "Not long. Probably just today," he says, clipping his answers.

The man studies him. Cobb senses he's wondering what kind of person rents a box truck and doesn't know which way he's going? No doubt the guy would like to ask another question but is having second thoughts.

"Well, safe travels to you," the man says at length, turning and walking away.

*

Judy hears the moped approach at high speed and steps into

the trees, and gets down. Jerry goes flying past her in a cloud of gravel dust back toward the cabin. Why was he going so fast? Is something wrong?

If he thinks he's got problems now, he'll be frantic in a few minutes, looking for her. She gets back on the gravel road and starts to jog. She needs to put some distance between herself and the cabin. Better yet, she needs to get out to the county road and flag somebody down before Jerry comes back the other way.

Minutes later she hears the moped return. There's no good place to take cover but she jumps into the tall grass by the roadside and lies flat. Jerry goes shooting past. About a hundred yards later, the moped goes into a skid, fishtails a little and stops. Jerry stands up and looks behind him. Did he see something? A bit of cloth? The reflection of a bracelet?

He walks the machine back a few steps, then bends down to pick up something in the road. She can't tell what it is – a candy wrapper, maybe. He pulls something black from his belt and looks around some more, then continues forward much more slowly and quietly. Jesus, is it a gun? He's really mad now. She has betrayed him.

He shifts into gear and resumes driving. She can barely hear the engine purring softly around the next bend. She'll have to be careful. He must think she's close. He's being cagey. She lies still for several minutes, lifting her head only a little to look and listen.

Did he ditch the bike to work his way back on foot and surprise her?

*

Shane emerges from the sheriff's office and heads for his car in the county parking lot. He's pissed and frustrated. The investigation has gone cold, and both the sheriff and county commissioner Biggs are unhappy about the pointless raid on the Buckley compound. State and county agencies have poured resources into a wild goose chase. Renting a helicopter isn't cheap. The sheriff's department is way over budget and, apparently, nowhere close to solving a crime that hasn't happened yet and may only be in Shane's imagination.

A white, county pickup truck pulls into the lot just as Shane reaches his vehicle. He recognizes the driver, who gets out and waves.

"Making your rounds, Harvey?" Shane asks. "Looks like you drew the short straw today."

"Yeah," Harvey says. "Rhododendron Park."

Shane gets into his vehicle and sits a second, then rolls down the window and leans his head out.

"Hey," he calls. "I could use some extra eyes and ears. Have you run across any box trucks when you were out and about the last few days?"

Harvey looks down at the ground a moment. "Not that come to mind offhand. Why do you ask?"

"I'm trying to find a Budget rental that I think was on the island a few days ago and has since vanished."

"Nothing like that," the county employee replies. "No Budget trucks."

"Do me a favor and let me know if you see one," Shane says, reaching into his wallet and handing the county employee his card. "Call my cell."

*

On the front porch of the inn, Brad, Shane and Robert nurse Corona beers and taco chips. They're mostly silent, alone with their thoughts. The rest of their party is out in the garden, doing plein air sketching and watercolors. Shane glances that way. They look relaxed and happy. That's good.

"I've just got nothing," Shane says. "How do you hide a Budget rental truck on this island?" He raises his beer and takes a sip from the glass bottle. "We know it's not at the Buckley compound."

Nobody speaks for half a minute.

"Unfortunately," Robert points out, "there are plenty of old barns where you could hide a truck."

Brad clears his throat. "Keep in mind, we don't even know if it's still here. Maybe it got off the island the night of the raid, before you got surveillance in place on the ferries and bridge."

"It's possible but they'd have to move awfully fast," Shane concedes. "We've issued a statewide be-on-the-lookout for it. But the island is my turf and if there's any chance it's still here, I've got to find it."

"Maybe," Brad continues, "we've been looking for the wrong

truck. We've been so focused on Budget, maybe they switched vehicles and the truck no longer says Budget."

Robert interjects, "He's right. There are plenty of other trucks in the world."

Shane's cell phone rings. He pulls it from his shirt pocket and looks at the display. It's an unknown number and he almost ignores it, but remembers he gave his card to the county employee a few hours earlier.

"I'd better take this," he tells Brad and Robert, getting up, turning his back and walking a few steps away.

"Judy!" he yells. "Oh thank god. Are you ok?"

Brad and Robert look up. Shane continues to talk for a few minutes, then ends the call and returns to his friends.

"She's safe. She escaped from where Jerry was holding her and is on her way here right now."

"Outstanding," Robert yells. "You'd better go tell Billy."

Minutes later, an old Chevy pickup truck pulls up to the inn and Judy gets out, thanking the driver profusely.

She runs up the steps and gives Billy a big hug, then does the same with all the others. She lingers when she gets to Robert and Marie. Shane hands Judy a beer and she sits down and starts to talk.

Chapter 15

"It's not a Budget truck," Judy says. "What I saw said Economy."

Robert looks at Brad. "You were right."

"I wonder how they did that," Shane says. He pulls out pictures of Raymond Cobb and Fred Franks. "Are these the men you saw hanging around the barn?" he asks.

"Yes," she replies. "This one especially scared me," pointing at Cobb. "Those eyes. He seemed barely able to control his anger. The whole time Jerry held me at the compound, I felt this guy was itching to put me away."

"Raymond Cobb," Brad says.

"Do you think Jerry knew you were a mole?" Shane asks.

"No, I think he just wasn't sure he could trust me. And those other guys definitely didn't trust me. It was a chance they couldn't take. Cobb – that's his name? – knew where I was. He could come over to the cabin at any moment and kill me. I'm certain that's what he wanted to do."

She explains that right after Robert and Marie entered the compound and found Judy, Jerry moved her to another location, a cabin in the woods near Possession Point and held her there until she escaped. Maybe they saved her in a way, because after that, Jerry had to assume Robert and Marie might have seen her and could connect her to the compound. She figured that out later. She never saw any more of the two men nor the truck.

"For the longest time I couldn't tell if Jerry was trying to protect me from his friends or get up the courage to kill me. He seemed to be struggling with that. Nobody knew where I was till you found me," Judy said, nodding to Robert and Marie. "So nobody could save me but myself. Several times a day Jerry left for about 45 minutes on his moped."

"So," Robert says, "assuming Jerry was going off to meet Cobb and Franks, which we can't know for sure, they were still on the island within a fairly small radius."

"Does Jerry know about me or that you have a son?"

"No," Judy says. "I didn't tell him a thing."

"You did well. Really well. Now, can you help us find Jerry's cabin?"

"I think so," Judy replies.

Brad, Shane, Robert and Judy pile into Brad's patrol car and head south. "When the nice people in the pickup drove me here I tried to remember which turns they made," Judy says. "But I was still shaking from not knowing if I'd ever get out of there alive."

Shane grabs his microphone and radios his office in Coupeville to report that Judy is safe and is leading him and an Idaho State Trooper friend to the cabin where she was held captive. He'll follow up with more information as soon as they determine the location.

About fifteen minutes south of Freeland, Judy directs Shane to turn right and continue south for several miles. At a major intersection at the bottom of a hill, she points left.

"It gets trickier from here," she says. "I'll have to look for landmarks."

"That's it," she says, pointing to a small driveway in the trees. Shane turns up it and they come to a gravel pit. Judging from the beer cans with holes in them, somebody's been doing target practice.

"Sorry," she says. "Go back to the road and drive a little farther. It's around here somewhere."

They drive out and take the next turn, which is another false start, and then the one after that. The third one is the right one. It's a long and winding forest lane. The cabin is tucked back in the trees — a perfect safe house.

"Heads up!" Shane exclaims. "Looks like he's here." He stops the vehicle. Jerry's car is parked under a tree in a spot that would be hard to see from the air.

"I don't think he's home," Judy says. "He was on the moped. He was just leaving the car here."

Shane and Robert both draw their service revolvers, separate from each other and approach the building in a crouch from two directions while Brad and Judy hang back at the car. Shane throws open the door, which is unlocked, while Robert covers him. Shane takes a moment to check it, then yells "Clear!" and signals for the others to come ahead.

Shane notes the window Judy used in her escape, which is still open. One end of the handcuffs is still locked to the bed. He looks at Judy. "You remembered that trick I taught you."

"I did."

"It appears Jerry didn't lose any time clearing out of here after he discovered you missing. I'm surprised he left his car."

"The moped is easier to conceal," Judy remarks.

"That's true," Shane agrees. "You mentioned that. Did you notice the color?"

"Fire-engine red."

Shane requests a team of officers to stake out the cabin in case Jerry comes back in the next twenty-four hours. He also alerts his office that Jerry was last seen on a red moped.

"I'm proud of you, Judy," Shane says, reaching out and hugging her. "This is the first real break we've had in days."

Judy smiles. She turns to Brad and Robert, and hugs both of them.

"Let's get you back to the inn so you can spend some time with Billy."

*

At Rhododendron Park, Raymond Cobb sits on a bench and clicks his pen nonstop against it. He jiggles his knee. He didn't like talking with that colored boy from the county. The guy's interest may have been entirely innocent but he was too nosy for comfort. Cobb studies his map. He needs to get off this island just as soon as possible.

He climbs into the cab, puts the key into the ignition and starts the engine. This is either a smart move or a dumb one – he isn't sure which. He slips the truck into gear and starts to drive out on the secluded camp road toward the highway. It's still daylight but he's got to take the risk. As much as possible, he'll stick to secondary roads. He knows he's just outside Coupeville, the county seat, which is headquarters of the sheriff's department. He still has to pass through

Oak Harbor, which no doubt has the largest police department on the island. It's a bad scenario – too many eyes and ears. Having double-crossed Jerry, he wonders if Jerry is still on board with the plan or whether Jerry has had second thoughts, turned himself in and cut a deal with the police. Jerry knows what Cobb's driving.

The other possibility is that Jerry and the girl have been caught. Cobb has an idea.

*

On the front deck of the inn, spirits are high as Judy recounts the story of her captivity, minus the details of what she did to pacify Jerry and save her own skin. Moose sits on her lap, Billy at her side. Robert and Marie tell their piece of it – hiking through dense woods to locate Judy and trigger Shane's big raid. Billy takes it all in with wide eyes – the sanitized version. He wants to know more about the helicopter. Shane makes him promise not to discuss what they're saying with anyone but the group.

Elizabeth invites Judy to stay the night – and probably longer – till Jerry is found and arrested. Shane agrees that it's much too dangerous for her to go home till they break the case. The inn is the safest place for her now.

Shane's cell phone rings and he gets up and steps away. It's another number he does not recognize, but he answers anyway.

"Detective?" a voice begins. "We talked the other day in the county parking lot and you gave me your card."

"Yes, that's right," Shane replies. "Harvey. What can I do for you?"

Harvey apologizes for disturbing Shane, which Shane assures him is alright. Harvey remembered something from his rounds at Rhododendron Park early this morning. It's probably nothing, he concedes, but it stuck in his mind.

"There was this guy on a bench at the park studying a map," Harvey says. "He didn't have a tent or anything, but was traveling in a box truck."

Shane stands up straight. "What kind of truck? Was it a Budget rental?"

"Well that's the thing," Harvey says. "I know you're looking for a Budget rental and this wasn't Budget. It was some other logo,

Thrift or something."

"Actually, it turns out I was wrong about Budget," Shane says. "I just learned that the two guys we're looking for are driving a truck that says Economy."

"That's it! That's what I saw in the park. But it wasn't two men. I only saw one."

"Can you describe the guy?" Shane says.

"White. Average build. Bald."

"Yeah."

"And tight-lipped."

"Yeah."

"Mean eyes."

"That's him," Shane declares – "one of the guys we're looking for."

"I used to live in the Midwest," Harvey says. "I've seen that look. This guy in the park was bad news. He hated me on sight."

Shane thanks him and punches the number for his office.

"One of our suspects with the box truck, Raymond Cobb, is camped at Rhododendron Park," Shane says. "Get some officers over there right now and seal off the park, and get the public out, but don't move in till I get there. He's a sharpshooter, and he's armed and highly dangerous. The truck may be a bomb. I'm on my way."

Shane and Robert grab their sidearms and rush to Shane's car. Brad piles into the back seat, not asking for permission. Shane turns on his red-and-blue lights and speeds out of the driveway, spraying gravel as he goes. The police radio already is alive with activity. Shane hits the siren.

Billy's jaw hangs open.

Chapter 16

By the time they reach the park, half a dozen sheriff's units already are deployed at the entrance, lights flashing. Two are black-and-gold SUVs, one is a green sedan with "Sheriff" across the entire side, and two others are black cruisers with light bars flashing red and blue. Shane drives past an EMT van, a mobile communications center and two Coupeville Town Marshall cars as he approaches the campground on the loop road. The first officer he meets gives him the news.

No box truck.

"Too late," Shane laments, pounding the steering wheel. "But we were close! Just hours behind him."

Cobb could easily be off the island by now, either on the Olympic Peninsula or the mainland. But Cobb has been cagey and Shane puts out an island-wide alert to all police agencies to be alert for a fleeing suspect, armed and dangerous, in an Economy box truck. He adds that the truck may be filled with explosives, so to exercise great caution when approaching the suspect.

*

Meanwhile, in a far corner of the Home Depot parking lot in Oak Harbor, Raymond Cobb makes some changes to his white truck. The Economy logo is now gone, replaced by the orange-and-white Home Depot logo. It looks nice and Home Depot is such a familiar name, he hopes it will deflect suspicion.

He got the Home Depot signage from a graphic design and printing studio. When he told the manager of the signage shop he worked for Home Depot and needed some temporary signage for a short-fuse job, the guy didn't challenge him or ask for ID. He just happily printed the signs – a nice sale and a foot in the door for possible future business with the corporate giant. The signs are big and pricey.

"Do you have a purchase order number for me?" the shop manager asked when it was time to pay.

"Honestly," Cobb said, "this is such a rush job my boss didn't have time for all that red tape. He just said 'get a receipt and bring it to me.'"

"No problem at all," the manager said. "We love cash."

Cobb handed him $500 in hundred dollar bills.

Cobb realized he might be paranoid in going to such lengths, but after the county employee talked to him at the park, he felt he couldn't be too careful. Better to keep everyone guessing. He congratulated himself on this idea to hide in plain sight, and decided to linger here till darkness before starting his run north across Deception Pass Bridge. He's betting the last thing a cop will check is a Home Depot truck in the Home Depot parking lot. The logo is so familiar to people he thinks it'll be his ticket to park unnoticed at quite a few locations in the city.

He hopes this store's employees won't question a truck that isn't part of their store's rental fleet. But do most even know? Still, it makes him a little nervous.

*

Jerry is screwed and knows it. Once Judy talks to the police, he will be fully implicated. In hindsight he should have listened to Cobb and Franks. By now Judy has poured out her story. His partners bailed from the safe house, cutting him out of the plot. He wonders now if he may be in their crosshairs. Cobb is a sharpshooter and Jerry is now a loose end. He knows what happens to loose ends.

He can't go back to the family compound because the sheriff is watching it. He can't go back to the safe house because Judy, he's pretty sure, has told them where it is. He's now wanted for kidnapping and is cut off from doing his live Facebook program any more. All he's got is a moped and a few dollars in his wallet, and he's wanted. Shit, shit, shit. He could call his dad, but not without putting him at risk. He needs to cut a deal – cut his losses, get some protection.

He knows people – old friends, losers and wannabe neo-Nazis – who might give him a few dollars and a bed for the night. But how far will that take him? This is a dead end. He pulls out his cell phone and punches some numbers.

"This is Jerry Buckley. I think you might be looking for me."

*

With time on his hands till nightfall, Cobb elects to get away from the truck and walk around the neighborhood for a while. He pulls his baseball cap low on his head and grabs a light windbreaker. A few blocks away, he enters a forlorn fast food shop, orders a burger, fries and a coke, and sits at a table watching obese employees serve exactly what he's eating to dozens of overweight customers. The place is dismal on a Friday night.

He eats half his fries, drinks half his coke, finishes the burger, uses the restroom, and tosses the leftovers of his meal and his free prize into the grimy garbage bin. Then he starts to walk through nearby neighborhoods, using up what's left of the daylight.

By the time he gets back to his truck, Home Depot is closed for the evening. The parking lot is quiet. He walks around back and removes the light bulb that illuminates his license plate. He smears some dirt on the plate, then returns to the cab, starts the engine, pulls forward and turns onto the highway, heading north. It's now or never. He sets his speed just shy of the limit. The grenade launcher is behind the seat. A terrycloth towel covers a Glock pistol on the passenger seat beside him.

Two miles north of the Navy base, Cobb drives past a police cruiser on the shoulder. His speed is under the limit and the officer, he assumes, is watching for erratic drivers or speeders. Neither of those scenarios is unusual close to a military base.

In the side mirror, Cobb watches the cruiser pull onto the highway some distance behind him. It closes the gap fast and his mirror lights up with red and blue flashing lights. He signals and pulls over to the roadside, stops, turns on his emergency flashers and unrolls the driver's side window.

"Sir," comes a voice on the cruiser's loudspeaker. "It looks like you have a light out on your license plate and it's dirty. I can't read it."

Cobb gets out and faces the cruiser's blinding spotlight. "Let me take a look," he yells. "This is a company truck." He walks back and bends down, makes a show of looking at it, then walks over to the cruiser as if to explain. The officer, a black man, rolls down his window. Without a word, Cobb reaches behind his back, swings his arm around with a gun and places a bullet between the officer's eyes.

Traffic is intermittent and nobody sees him make the move. Cobb leaves the officer sitting in the car, engine idling, with the headlights on. Within minutes somebody will find the policeman and this stretch of highway will be crawling with cops.

He takes the next exit and heads out into the countryside. He'll spend the night in the truck, off the road in some dark, quiet place.

*

Shane's pager goes off, alerting him to check his radio. When he turns it on, a full police emergency is in progress. An officer is down north of Oak Harbor.

Sheriff's officers, Oak Harbor police, Navy police and state patrol all are responding to the scene on the main north-south highway. Shane yells to Brad and Robert in the parlor. They join him in his study and listen as police close the highway and begin an area-wide manhunt. Deception Pass Bridge is closed. Police place roadblocks on the highway both directions from the scene and search all vehicles.

Shane calls his office and learns the details, a single bullet between the eyes.

Unfortunately, the officer hadn't been able to relay much information. He'd radioed his dispatcher he was pulling over a commercial truck to alert the driver to an equipment issue – a light out on the license plate, and that the plate was unreadable because it was dirty. When dispatch attempted to follow up minutes later, the officer did not respond. Another officer drove to the location to check and found his colleague deceased at the wheel. Investigating officers recovered a shell casing that had rolled under the car.

"Cobb?" Brad asks.

"I'm almost certain," Shane says.

With the north end of the island crawling with police, and

Shane an hour away, there isn't much he can add to the effort at this time. With luck, he believes, the manhunt will find Cobb and recover the truck, and by morning he can go back to his vacation in peace after he takes care of one other thing.

Jerry Buckley has turned himself in and wants to talk about a deal. Shane plans to interview him first thing in the morning in the county jail at Coupeville.

*

Elizabeth, Irene, Marie and Judy are up early the next morning, preparing a hearty breakfast, when the first of the men appear. Judy is working on a skillet of hash browns and eggs. Marie is setting the table.

"Could you use some help?" Robert asks. "This scene has a bad, sexist look about it."

"I think we've got this," Elizabeth says. "Pour a cup of coffee and sit down. You can help later with the cleanup."

Robert thinks he just got snookered. "Is Brad up yet?"

"He didn't sleep well," Irene says. "He's moving a little more slowly." Elizabeth looks at her with knowing eyes. Irene flashes the "cut" hand signal to her and Elizabeth instantly changes the subject.

"Shane was up half the night monitoring the situation up north," Elizabeth says. "So far they haven't found the guy."

"It's only a matter of time now," Robert says.

Irene crosses the room to the range and puts a hand lightly on Judy's back. "Nice to see you smiling this morning."

"I can't tell you how relieved I am to be waking up here," Judy says. "Jerry's in custody and I just took my first hot shower in about a week.

"And," she adds, "you've all been very gracious and welcoming to me."

Shane is rubbing his red eyes when he enters the room. His tall frame sags under the weight of exhaustion and worry, and little sleep. His hair is a haystack. He nods to Judy. Elizabeth sets a cup of coffee on the table for him and he sits down next to Robert, raises the cup to his mouth and sips. Then he puts the cup down, turns to Robert and confesses, "Things aren't adding up."

"Such as?"

"Where's Fred Franks, the bomb-maker? Based on what the county employee observed, Cobb was alone in the truck at Rhododendron Park. And he was also apparently alone when that trooper stopped the truck north of Oak Harbor."

"Maybe Jerry can shed some light on this when you talk to him this morning," Robert says.

"Jerry's an accessory to murder now," Shane points out. "He has all the reason he needs to spill everything he knows."

"By the way," Shane continues, "where's Brad?"

"Still sleeping," Irene replies.

"Is he slowing down?" Shane asks. "Is he ok?"

"Oh you know," Irene says, pursing her lips and shrugging. "Ask him sometime."

*

After breakfast, Shane and Robert clear the table and wash the dishes, then leave the women and Brad to a morning of art classes in the garden while they head north to meet with Jerry at the jail.

Jerry is wearing an orange jumpsuit and handcuffs when the guard leads him into the interview room. A public defender already is seated at the table and a tape recorder sits at the center of the table. "I'm turning on this recorder," Shane announces. He and Robert introduce themselves.

"You can take those off," Shane says to the guard, nodding toward the handcuffs. Shane turns to the public defender. "I understand your client would like to discuss a deal."

"That's right."

"I'll explain the situation and then let's hear what he has to give us." Shane looks at Jerry and explains, "One of our officers was shot and killed last night on a traffic stop north of Oak Harbor. We're pretty sure one of your associates was the shooter, and once we prove it, that'll make you an accessory to murder."

Jerry's expression falls.

Shane continues, "You're involved in a conspiracy that could take a lot of lives. You kidnapped a woman and held her for several days at your family compound. That implicates your parents. The kidnap victim is working with us now. Your own mother delivered meals to her during captivity. So you'd better have something useful

135

for me."

"I'll tell you everything I know," Jerry says, "if you'll take the death penalty off the table and keep my parents out of it, and let me talk to Judy, and keep me away from the general prison population."

"Anything else?" Shane asks. "A dish of M&Ms for your cell? I can't guarantee anything," Shane says. "If your information is solid, I'll take your cooperation into account and will do all I can to honor your requests."

"We need more than that," the public defender objects.

"Sorry," Shane says. "That's all you're getting from me. And if things go south because your client didn't cooperate, I guarantee this is going to be bad for him."

Jerry starts to talk. He met Fred Franks and Raymond Cobb on an Internet chat site three months ago and indicated he wanted to take some direct action beyond protests and marches. They came out from the Midwest for the memorial protest at the state park, and together the three of them developed a plan to bomb a prominent target.

"What's the target?" Shane asks.

"We discussed a long list of transportation systems, courthouses and federal buildings. I know Fred cased several buildings on the mainland, including the Federal Building in Seattle. But he never told me specifically which one he had chosen; he's very cagey about revealing what he's thinking. But we talked about sending a letter afterwards from a black militant group taking credit for the bombing, to incite white backlash."

That's a new twist on an old theme, Shane thinks.

"The two of them didn't take me fully into their confidence, I think because of my girlfriend. They weren't sure how much she might find out from me. They wanted me to get rid of her permanently."

Shane nods. "So where are they headed now?"

"I don't know. After the raid we got out of the compound fast and split up to two safe houses. I took Judy with me and confined her at my location while delivering meals to Cobb and Franks at their hideout. The plan was to lie low for a few days till the search went dead, but when I went to their safe house yesterday morning they were already gone – didn't tell me a thing."

"So then what?"

"I raced back to my own place and Judy was gone. She'd escaped and they'd left me high and dry."

Shane and Robert exchange glances.

"Did they finish mixing the explosive?" Robert asks.

"Yes," Jerry replies. "Just barely, before the raid."

"How did they rig it to go off?" Robert asks. "With a timer?"

"No," Jerry says. "Cobb showed me a grenade launcher. I don't know exactly what he's going to do. I assume if you hit a truckload of explosives with a grenade, you have your detonation."

"Holy shit," Robert exclaims.

Jerry fidgets and looks down at his hands. "They won't hesitate to kill me if they get the chance. Or have someone do it for them once I'm locked up. You've got to keep me away from the general prison population."

Shane asks for the location of Cobb and Franks' safe house and Jerry provides it.

"I'll get back to you about your terms," Shane tells him, standing. Robert gets up as well, and together they walk out in silence.

In the parking lot, Robert remarks, "I don't think he knows Cobb and Franks have split up."

Shane agrees. "And it begs the question, where is Franks and what is he doing? Did Cobb send him back to take care of Jerry and Judy?"

"If the bomb is complete, maybe he's gone home and left Cobb to detonate it."

"I doubt it," Shane says. He calls his office to report that in addition to the gun that killed the patrol officer, and a truckload of explosives, the suspect is also believed to be armed with a grenade launcher.

*

Robert and Shane find the safe house – a combination hay barn and chicken coop – where Jerry said it would be. It's so far off a private road, at the edge of a small farm clearing, it's easy to see how Franks and Cobb were able to drop out of sight and conceal the truck.

The two officers examine the scene and Shane calls for a

forensic team to process it for evidence. "I'll have someone come back and take a plaster casting of the tire tracks in the barn," Shane says. "Then we can tie this place to the truck when we find it."

There's little to see but chickens pecking at something gray and dead on the ground in the barn – the remains of a rodent or some animal droppings, maybe some spoiled luncheon meat, Shane assumes.

Meanwhile, there's been no progress in the big search north of Oak Harbor for the person who shot the patrol officer. Shane continues to believe it was Raymond Cobb, but can't rule out one hundred percent the possibility it was someone else. Once again, the box truck has vanished and Shane assumes Cobb has gone into deep cover.

They are no closer than ever to knowing what Cobb's target is, nor where Franks has gone.

When they get back to the lodge they find the others relaxed and happy, sketching in the garden. Judy puts down her sketch pad and goes to meet Shane, eager to know about his visit with Jerry. For the sake of the investigation and future prosecution, Shane chooses his words carefully.

"He's cooperative," Shane says, "and concerned for his own safety. He'd like to see you. I told him I'd get back to him about that. You're under no obligation to talk to him and it's not a good idea to do it just yet. If I were you I wouldn't do it at all."

"He could have killed me," Judy says, "but he didn't."

"If you hadn't gotten away I think he would have," Shane says. "He was involved in something ugly that would have taken a lot of lives, and still could. He's going away for a long time, probably the rest of his life, and I think you should get him out of your life totally and forever."

"Oh god," Judy says, sinking into a chair and holding her head in both hands.

*

Deep in the trees, three miles from where Cobb shot the officer, the fugitive sleeps fitfully in the cab of the truck. The spot he chose is well off the road, under some trees, hidden from the air. That's good because a helicopter with a searchlight flew over his location twice during the night. The search is hot and will remain so for at least twenty-four hours, he thinks. He won't make a move till it quiets down.

Even then, he suspects, police will be watching the bridge.

Shooting the cop made everything worse, he realizes, but once the guy pulled him over there was no choice. If the officer had given the dispatcher his plate number, it would have come up as stolen.

Getting across the bridge now is going to be almost impossible.

*

Judy and Marie watch from the deck as a sailboat silently rides the breeze in the distance. The warm afternoon, birds chirping and squirrels chattering, lulls them both into a trance. Marie fights to stay awake. With effort she makes conversation.

"How does it feel to be out of there?"

"Suddenly the world feels like a very beautiful place. For several days there, I wasn't sure I'd ever get the chance to see Billy again. Or enjoy the simple pleasures of sitting on a deck like this and smelling the flowers."

"This is so relaxing," Judy says, "after those tense days and nights at the compound. I couldn't tell what Jerry was going to do with me and I don't think he knew, either. But those two men knew what they wanted him to do."

"You did well," Marie says. "I can't imagine what was going through your mind."

"I just wanted to survive," Judy says. "Did some things to buy time that I really didn't want to do."

*

"Don't you have children, Officer Lindstrom?" the old woman asks.

"We're not here to talk about me," Shane replies.

Ida Mae Buckley sits in the back seat of Shane's cruiser, a mile down the road from the compound. From camera surveillance he knows her routine – that she drives to the store every Thursday afternoon for groceries. He knew he could pick her up today, alone, without her husband's knowledge, if he waited for this moment.

"Well if you had children," she continues, "you'd know that when a son or daughter needs your help, you help them."

"He's not a child, Mrs. Buckley. He's a grown man and he's responsible for his actions. You and your husband knew he was holding that woman in the compound against the law. You aided and abetted him in the federal crime of kidnapping. That's a very serious matter."

She sets her jaw and glares at him.

"Are you arresting me?"

"No, right now we're having a little chat and I'm assessing whether you're going to cooperate with us."

"Because I am not in good health. I am old and have high blood pressure, and heart trouble. If you arrest me I'm afraid the stress will kill me. I need to tell my husband where I am, and I need a doctor."

"Speaking of your husband," Shane goes on, "let's talk about the meals you made for your husband to deliver to Jerry at a dead drop after he fled the compound. I think your husband knew Jerry was involved in something very serious."

"I did what any mother would do who loves her son, and that's all my husband did, too."

"You knew exactly what you were doing, both of you," Shane explains. "You were assisting a fugitive running from the law."

"I don't know what you think Jerry and his friends did. I just made sandwiches."

*

The explosion is horrific. Windows shatter in a spray of glass on nearby houses and buildings. Car alarms go off. A propane tank shoots into the sky like a rocket, trailing sparks, and tumbles end-over-end back to earth two blocks away, demolishing a house. Black smoke billows into the night sky, illuminated by a tower of orange flames.

Residents eight miles away feel the concussion and call the Navy base to ask if a military jet has crashed in the city. No aircraft are missing, but the orange glow on the horizon seems to confirm the worst.

Raymond Cobb drapes a blanket over his grenade launcher and

walks calmly to his truck three blocks away, carrying the bundle in his arms. He gets in, sets the weapon behind the seat, turns the key and starts to drive.

Police, fire engines and ambulances speed toward him, lights flashing and sirens screaming. He signals and pulls to the shoulder, and they race by, disappearing to the south in his rear view mirror. No one is looking for a guy in a Home Depot truck tonight.

Large crowds of onlookers already are rushing to the scene to watch a spectacle like nothing they've ever witnessed.

At home at the inn, Shane's pager goes off. He switches on his police radio and is not prepared for what he hears. He calls Robert and Brad from the living room.

"Apparently Raymond Cobb has struck," he declares.

"Where?" Robert adds.

"Oak Harbor. There's been a huge explosion at a propane storage facility and witnesses think they saw something streak toward the tank at ground level and hit it. It sounds like a rocket-propelled grenade."

"Dear god," Brad exclaims. "Fatalities?"

"It looks that way," Shane says. "The explosion devastated a wide area and flattened at least one house. Emergency crews just got there and don't know just how bad it was yet."

"And the truck bomb?" Robert asks.

"We don't know yet."

"I sure didn't expect that," Robert says.

In the cab of his truck on this pleasant summer evening, Cobb whistles a happy tune as he drives. The explosion was quite a show, a nice rehearsal of bigger things to come. He loves watching things blow up. Now, with not a single police car going his direction, he drives through Deception Pass State Park, across the bridge and off the island.

*

Shane is up early the next morning for an update on developments in Oak Harbor. He wanders into the kitchen and starts the coffeemaker, then turns on a small TV in the room at low volume. Oak Harbor is the lead story on the Northwest news, eclipsing preparations for a large civil rights march to be held on

Seattle's Capitol Hill. Police expect up to 100,000 people for the march. Meanwhile, police on Whidbey Island say the explosion in Oak Harbor is possibly linked to white militant separatists. Fox News commentators are calling the reports a witch hunt to discredit conservatives, timed to draw attention to the fake civil rights march in Seattle, as well as the administration in the nation's capitol.

In Oak Harbor three people are dead in the house that was flattened. Several others are hospitalized with injuries. A reporter stands in front of the rubble and interviews a witness who believes she saw something streak low across the ground toward the storage tank just before it exploded. No one saw Cobb or his truck, though police are calling him a suspect.

Brad shows up and joins Shane in front of the TV. Shane reaches for two coffee mugs, sets them on the counter and pours one for each of them.

"Rough night," Brad says, picking up his cup, shaking his head and turning away from the TV.

"You?" Shane asks.

"No, I mean you with everything that happened last night."

"You can say that again. The last thing I expected with our focus on the truck bomb was something like this."

"What was the point of it?" Brad asks.

"That's what troubles me. It has nothing to do with anything. Maybe he just wanted to show us what he could do."

"Or, you know," Brad suggests, "maybe blowing up a propane storage facility was the means to a different end."

"What do you mean?"

"Maybe it was a diversion. After shooting that patrol officer, Cobb was pretty well pinned down by police surveillance. He was smart enough to know he couldn't get off the island. But an urban catastrophe like that scrambles everything and ties up all the police in one place."

"That makes sense," Shane allows. "What better time to slip off the island than when everyone is racing to the scene of a disaster somewhere else?"

"If that's what he did, then we still have an active threat of a truck bomb," Brad says, "but now it has probably moved to the mainland."

They sit in silence for a moment. Shane wonders if now is the time, and finally begins, "I've been wanting to ask you about something else."

Brad nods.

"You and I have been friends longer than any of the others in this group – longer than Robert and Marie, longer even than Elizabeth and me."

"That's true," Brad agrees. "We've been through some things."

"You've seemed a little preoccupied on this vacation, not your usual self. Tired, maybe. I wanted to ask if you're feeling ok."

"Oh you know. Age," Brad laughs. "Time catches up with a guy."

"I don't think you're leveling with me."

"Jesus, Shane, that's a little direct."

"I'm a cop. I have radar for bullshit."

Slowly and softly, Brad begins to talk. At first, he says, he didn't want his problems to be the focus of this reunion, which should be a joyous time. Then the whole situation with Jerry Buckley and Judy broke out, and he didn't want to burden Shane when so much else was weighing on him.

To make it short, Brad says, he had a cold that wouldn't go away. He was tired and rundown. When the sweats and fevers started, he saw a doctor. One thing led to another – test after test. Hodgkins Lymphoma was finally diagnosed just before he and Irene left on this trip.

"Are you scared?" Shane asks.

"Well sure, a little," Brad admits. "This is entirely new territory for me. They tell me my odds are good, but I have some hurdles to cross. I need an infusion port installed in my chest. I will need to get through six months of chemotherapy without complications messing up the infusion schedule. Then, on top of that, I could use a little luck."

"I hear you," Shane says.

"And I worry about Irene. If I don't make it, what happens to her and the ranch, and Bolivar? She's looking at big changes in her life – giving up the life we've made together and entering a new phase."

"That's understandable."

"On the other hand, why should I worry or be sad?" Brad asks. "I've lived seventy good years. Everyone dies of something, so if this is what gets me, I should only feel grateful for the wonderful life I've had and the wonderful friends."

"Do you think about Stu and the choices he made?" Shane is referring to Brad's best friend who accompanied him from Idaho to Whidbey Island several years ago to investigate Bella's death, only to reveal he had Leukemia. On the way home from that trip, Stu nosedived his airplane into Lake Chelan and committed suicide.

"A lot," Brad admits. "This is giving me some idea of what was going through his mind that whole time."

"I think he was a little too quick to give up," Shane says. "I feel optimistic that you're going to come out of this okay and we'll be celebrating with you next summer. I really feel that. But either way, no matter what happens, you have some good people in your corner who will be with you every step of the way."

"I'm sorry to lay this on you," Brad says.

"You know, I feel better now that you've told me. Our friendship means more than any of this other stuff," Shane says, waving his arm in the air. "Criminals come and go, and there's always another. Real friends are rare, and when we find one, we need them for life."

Chapter 17

Cobb snores in the cab of his truck in LaConner's wooded Pioneer Park, just across the arch bridge from the Indian reservation. After crossing Deception Pass Bridge from Whidbey Island last night in darkness, he stuck to the back roads to minimize chances of detection. Just east of the big oil refineries on the outskirts of Anacortes he took a right turn onto the reservation. He needed a restroom, saw the sign for this pocket park, and was pretty sure it would have one.

He stirs and sits up in the cab, blinking his eyes. Daylight is just starting and his stomach rumbles with hunger. It's been 24 hours since his last meal. He opens the door, steps out and looks around. This is a day-use park and it seems unlikely he'll have any company for many hours. He pees next to the truck, locks the doors, then starts to explore.

Within minutes he finds a well-worn foot trail under the orange bridge that leads in the direction of town and, he hopes, someplace to get breakfast.

LaConner is obviously a tourist town, located on the banks of a picturesque channel lined with boats. The tourist shops are closed at this early hour and the streets are empty except for a few cars in front of a storefront a block in the distance.

He makes his way quickly to the location, opens the weathered door with a *ding* and steps inside to the aroma of coffee, bacon and eggs. Half a dozen people in overalls and checkered shirts sit at the counter and at a table in the window. He's not prepared for the two state patrol officers at a table in the back corner. They're talking and don't even look up from their breakfasts. He pulls his baseball cap lower on his forehead.

For an instant he considers turning around and walking out. Instead, he crosses the room and pulls out a chair about six feet from the police table, positioning himself with the officers mostly at his back. The waitress drops a menu in front of him. He turns his coffee cup upright and she fills it with black coffee, spilling a little in the saucer and daubing it up with a napkin.

"I'd like this one, 'The Barnyard,'" he tells her, "scrambled, with sausage, hash browns and toast," pointing to number one on the menu, "and ketchup."

"You got it," she replies, taking back the menu and retreating toward the kitchen with her pot of coffee.

He sits there alone, waiting, staring into space, catching bits of conversation. "Never saw it coming . . . up half the night with that explosion . . . hell of a mess."

Cobb turns in his chair toward the officers. "Excuse me," he begins, "I couldn't help overhearing a little. Did something happen?"

"Big explosion and fire last night in Oak Harbor," one of the troopers says. "Long night. Three dead. All hands on deck."

"My god," Cobb says.

"And one of our officers was killed on a traffic stop earlier," the other one says.

"Good lord, did they get the guy?"

"Not yet. But we've got the whole state screwed down tight."

"Any idea what he's driving?"

"Just a commercial truck. We think it's an Economy rental, but that's about all."

"Is there a description of the guy?"

"Yeah," one of the officers says with a note of sarcasm. "Average height, medium build, clean shaven."

"That could be anyone," Cobb says, shrugging his shoulders.

"Yeah," the officer replies. "It could be you."

Nobody says anything for a heartbeat. Then the officer cracks a smile and breaks into a laugh, and Cobb joins in.

"You had me there," Cobb says. "But I'm not clean shaven," rubbing the stubble of two days' growth. "I hope you find the guy. I'll keep an eye out."

The waitress returns with two plates balanced on her arm, and a plastic squeeze bottle of ketchup. She sets all of it down, puts Cobb's check on the corner of the table and walks away.

Cobb eats fast and cleans everything from his plates. The two troopers are still talking behind him.

He glances at the check, tucks a $20 bill under his coffee cup, pushes back his chair and walks out into the morning, letting the door swing shut behind him.

This little tourist haven really isn't where he wants to spend the day but it might be a good place to hide in plain sight. It sounds like the search for him is way too hot. No one is especially likely to notice the truck in the park for a few hours.

*

With Jerry in custody and talking, and Cobb obviously northbound in the truck, Shane is completely baffled about the disappearance of suspect number two, Fred Franks. The truck is Shane's chief worry and Cobb is driving it. The statewide manhunt for Cobb is so intensive Shane thinks it's only a matter of time till they find him. But where is Franks and what is he doing?

It crosses his mind that the whole focus on Cobb could be another diversion. Maybe the propane explosion and Cobb's breakout to the north are intended to divert resources from the real threat, which is Franks. He wonders if Cobb and Franks are smart enough to plan such an elaborate diversion, sending all of law enforcement on a rabbit chase for nothing.

Maybe there are no explosives in the truck at all; maybe they're somewhere else. Cobb and Franks were alone at that safe house for a couple of days. Maybe they hatched a surprise. Maybe Franks is headed west on the Port Townsend Ferry or east to Mukilteo and Seattle.

Shane would know a lot more if he could find Cobb and get a look inside that truck. Because if it isn't rigged as a bomb, then the bomb is somewhere else and he can't afford to let it reach its destination.

*

Jerry sits in the interview room in his orange jumpsuit, chained to a floor bolt, staring at his hands. The door opens and Judy walks in. Shane insists on the chains as a condition of allowing her to be alone with him in the room, and Shane watches now on a closed-circuit monitor just outside.

"Hi babe," Judy greets Jerry as she closes the door behind her. Judy walks over and gives him a light kiss on the top of the head. The casual intimacy grates on Shane and he doesn't know why. "Are they treating you ok?"

"I can't complain." He smiles sheepishly and she smiles back almost flirtatiously. She tosses her hair. And winks.

"Damn," Jerry says.

"I heard you wanted to see me."

"Look," he continues, "I'm sorry about all this. Sorry I dragged you into it. Things got way more complicated than I ever foresaw."

"How could you do it? You almost got me killed."

"I was stupid."

Shane senses that even after everything that happened, Judy and this creepy racist share a connection – chemistry or something. There's an attraction, puppy love or physical lust or something. Jerry represents excitement to her, an element of risk.

Shane pictures what went on between Judy and this guy behind closed doors. The thought sickens him, that the mother of his son could debase herself that much.

Even though Shane has never been happier than he is now with Elizabeth, on some level he still has feelings, certainly compassion, for this reckless and impulsive woman who dresses way below her age. Whatever he's watching in that room, if it isn't real, Judy is a better actress than he thought.

Judy sits quietly, not speaking, giving Jerry time to form his thoughts.

"Are you ok?" Jerry asks. "Something wrong?"

"I've been better," she replies, playing him like a pro. "I can't go home."

"Why not?"

"Because the cops haven't caught either of your accomplices and I'm afraid they could yet come back and silence me."

"Oh god," Jerry moans. "I don't know. Cobb is the one who scares me. He's the shooter, the cold-blooded one. I don't see Franks doing that. He's all about the bomb – loves that bloody bomb too much."

"You know they've split up," Judy says.

"I heard that."

"So why didn't Franks stay with the bomb?"

"I don't know. I've tried to figure that out. When I discovered them missing from the safe house I figured I was in danger, too.

"You don't think they're pulling some stunt, do you? Like using the truck as a diversion with a fake bomb while Franks delivers the real bomb somewhere else?"

"If they are, it sure isn't anything they discussed around me. But Cobb is capable of anything."

Judy lets the thought sit for a while.

"Capable of killing his partner, Franks?"

"Holy shit," Jerry says, looking up at the ceiling. "Holy shit."

It's a thought Shane hadn't really considered – that Cobb is in fact now a lone wolf. If so, then Cobb may be the only one who can clear up what happened to Franks – who can lead them to the body. They'll have to take him alive to have any hope of resolving that question. Given Cobb's propensity for violence, and the fact that he killed a trooper, Shane thinks he knows how any standoff with lawmen will end.

*

With the search for Cobb now centered off-island, Shane's direct role is mostly over. There's a sense of relief back at the lodge, where activity turns to preparations for Billy's birthday, with Elizabeth and Judy coordinating the balloons and party hats.

Marie, whose reputation as a baker is formidable, accepts the assignment of baking a cake topped with chocolate and vanilla frosting rocks, "something I've never attempted before," she admits. "Conglomerate will be the fun one," she says.

Shane thinks Brad is coming to life, smiling and joking now, after finally getting his secret off his chest. It is good to see him back in old form. The shift in the mood is good for them all.

But Shane is thinking about the safe house where Jerry last saw Cobb and Franks together. He pulls Robert aside and suggests, "Let's run up there and take one more look."

They excuse themselves for an hour and leave in Shane's Suburban.

At the barn nothing has changed. "The chickens have finished their work," Robert observes out loud. "The dead thing on the ground is gone, pecked to smithereens." The two men walk around the room, looking atop ledges and into stalls, behind doors, anyplace they might have missed something – a tin can, cigarette, shell casing .

. .

Finally, out of boredom, Robert takes his boot and shoves at the compressed hay where Cobb and Franks must have slept, poking at it, shifting it around.

"Wait a minute," he remarks. "Might have something here."

He reaches down and retrieves a crumpled piece of paper, which he unfolds. It's a color copy of a photograph – of a building. Shane doesn't recognize it. "If it's around here, someone at the office may know what it is," he says.

The trouble is there's no way to know if Cobb and Franks lost the piece of paper, discarded it as no longer important, or planted it deliberately as a misleading clue.

"Good work," Shane tells Robert. "Let's run up to my office."

Chapter 18

The building in the picture turns out to be the federal courthouse in Seattle. Shane didn't recognize the camera angle. It's already under heightened security as one of the most prominent, high-value terrorist targets in the area. Shane can't imagine Cobb would choose such a well-defended target, but obviously he and Franks were carrying a picture of it.

An hour away in LaConner, as the daytime crowds grow, Cobb walks around town and wonders about all the normal people with little on their minds – people with shopping bags and lattes, bored husbands trailing their wives, people sitting at sidewalk tables, smiling and laughing, taking selfies with their iPhones.

He buys an ice cream cone and walks over to the water's edge to eat it where he can watch boats in the channel. This might be the last normal day of his life. The truth is that life had been anything but normal, thanks to his dad. The memories have followed Cobb everywhere he's gone.

The beatings started when he was old enough to remember. After his mom and sister left, before Cobb even started school, his dad mostly drank and whipped Cobb and his sister with the buckle end of a belt. She'd been his protector and he'd tried to be hers. Terror, pain and arbitrary cruelty focused the mind, he learned early. He knew no other way to get what he wanted than through pain – by inflicting it.

He wore long pants and shirts to school even on warm days to hide the welts and bruises. If social workers noticed and came to the house, his dad would beat him even more.

His school years in Indiana were a blur – mostly of paddlings, trips to the principal's office for fighting and bullying, and expulsion.

The Marines taught him a skill – how to kill – and he'd been honing his craft ever since. The separatist movement became his community and he surrounded himself with others who shared the same need – to have enemies.

He wanted to do one big thing before he died, something that would put his name in the books for others to read and remember, like the guy who died in the battle with federal agents on Whidbey. He had always felt like an outsider. But with a new president in the White House and a shift in the political climate, the winds were blowing his way a little more. The president openly said what everyone privately knew – that immigrants, slum-dwellers and people of color were ruining this country. They were the problem – rapists and terrorists and drug addicts. Patriots like Cobb and those who thought like him might not be such bad people after all.

But all the "normal" people walking around LaConner today with their lattes and shopping bags are asleep, Cobb thinks, oblivious to the underground war a few patriots like him are fighting to take back their country. Have they ever done anything heroic in their lives? He highly doubts it. This will wake them up.

*

"Where do you suppose he is right this moment?" Marie asks as she sits with Shane, Brad and Robert on the inn's front porch and looks out at two deer grazing on the lush lawn. Baby Martin sleeps in her lap. Elizabeth, Irene, Judy and Billy sketch birds in the back yard.

"Yearling bucks," Brad remarks.

"What?"

"Those deer. The males stick together for a couple of years before going their separate ways. But what was the question again?"

"Where is he right now?"

Shane looks up from his newspaper. "I think he's holed up somewhere in a separatist safe house, waiting for the heat to die down. What about you, Robert?"

"Parked in the woods somewhere, waiting for darkness."

"And you, Brad?" Shane asks.

"Devil's advocate. I think he's hidden in plain sight, out in the open. But we don't see him because he has tricked us into looking for the wrong thing."

"How do you come up with that?"

"He had us looking for a Budget rental, when actually he had changed the signage to Economy. You reviewed hours of webcam video from all over the area and none of the cameras picked up an Economy truck. So I think he has already changed it again."

"It's an interesting thought," Robert allows. "He can't go forever living in the shadows, napping in the cab, without eating. Maybe he isn't hiding at all. He's off island by now. Maybe he's sitting in a café or tavern somewhere, living large. Or a casino. People expect him to be hiding. Maybe he's doing the opposite."

"Okay," Brad says. "Let's build a scenario. He sets off a big explosion after dark in Oak Harbor and, in the resulting chaos, drives off the island. His destination is the Federal Building in Seattle, for lack of another lead. He wants to lie low in daylight and stay off the highly patrolled highways with all their video cameras. Where would he be now?"

"On the back roads, on a line from Deception Pass to Seattle," Shane says, "Swinomish Reservation, LaConner, Fir Island, Stanwood, Silvana, Smokey Point. That's how I'd go."

"Wanna drive over there and look around?" Robert asks. "It's like looking for a needle in a haystack, but it's better than sitting here fretting about it."

Shane looks at Brad. "Do you want to go with us, Brad? You're the scenario guy."

"I'm tempted to say yes," he replies, "but I think this is best left to the pros. I'll stay here with the rest of the group. I can handle a gun in case Fred Franks shows up, which I don't expect."

"I'll leave one for Marie, too," Shane says.

Shane and Robert round up their supplies, including some extra clips for their guns, a set of walkie-talkies and two bulletproof vests. In the trunk, Shane places a rifle and a shotgun. He assures Elizabeth, "I'll call when we get over there and let you know where we are and when we'll be back." He gives her a long hug and a kiss. Robert and Marie do the same.

"Stay safe," Elizabeth says.

*

After passing the whole morning in town, looking at everything there is to see and buying a couple of deli sandwiches to go, Cobb takes the trail under the bridge back to his truck.

The sight of a LaConner town police car in the deserted park, jolts him like a bucket of cold water. Peering through the passenger side window of his cab is a uniformed officer, an older guy, gray hair, moving slowly, with an ample belly over his belt. Citizens patrol, perhaps.

"This your truck?" the cop asks.

"Yes it is."

"You can't park here all day. We get folks sleeping in the park and it makes parents uncomfortable for their kids. This is really a picnic area."

"I'm sorry," Cobb says. "I drove in here to use the restroom. The place was dead quiet. I took a little break and noticed the trail to town, and thought it looked like a nice walk."

"It's a pretty morning for it," the officer says. "Can't say that I blame you."

"This is a nice town," the driver says, "Shame about the eyesore."

"What eyesore?"

"That Indian reservation you have to look at."

"I think they were here first," the cop says. "Penning them up on a reservation wasn't their idea."

Cobb shrugs. "Maybe they wouldn't be there if they had some ambition. I'll get on my way with the truck."

The cop's affable smile vanishes. "Yeah, I think it might be best if you to do that."

Cobb gets in, starts the engine and backs up to turn around. The officer walks toward the restrooms. Cobb hesitates.

He wonders what the officer saw, whether he was curious about anything like the license plate or the cling signage. Probably not, but it's a loose end and he doesn't like loose ends.

*

Driving through a tunnel of trees, Robert becomes aware that he and Shane have entered another world. The tunnel gives way to a breathtaking view left and right, and hundreds of feet down, as they start across Deception Pass Bridge. "This may be a wild goose chase," he says, "but it's a scenic one."

"You're on vacation," Shane points out. "Try to enjoy it between shootouts."

"I think my shootout days are over," Robert says. "I've applied for an opening as the governor's driver."

"Seriously?"

"Scout's honor. I've interviewed with him and we hit it off, so I think I have a good shot at it."

"That's wonderful."

"Yeah, now that I'm a family man, Marie wants me to tone it down a notch and concentrate on staying alive."

"Gosh, I hope you get it. But don't tell Elizabeth. I need to do the very same thing."

"You've got your inn," Robert says. "That's a pretty attractive retirement plan, and Elizabeth is a pretty attractive partner to share it with."

"That's what I'm thinking, too. So," Shane continues, "you and Marie are settling into the Idaho lifestyle?"

"We are."

"I sure liked what I saw of the state last summer."

"We love the state and we really like Boise. It's a clean, progressive city with a good arts community and a university, and parks and public spaces. Plenty of outdoor recreation. Skiing nearby at Bogus Basin and Sun Valley in the wintertime."

They ride in silence for a few minutes, passing two small lakes on the left where anglers in small boats and rafts sit and wait on a peaceful morning.

"Before our day gets too busy," Shane begins, "there's something I think you might want to know about Brad. He's going to be spending some time in Boise over the next year. You and Marie may be in a good position to offer some moral support to both Brad and Irene."

Just west of Anacortes, Shane turns right, onto Reservation Road, a narrow, secondary route through mostly second-growth forest toward the Swinomish tribal community and LaConner. "This is absolutely the way I would go if I were trying to stay off the interstate," he says.

Robert watches driveways and dirt roads flash by on the right and left, thinking any one of them could conceal a truck. After a few minutes, the forest gives way to a settlement of tribal buildings nestled along a picturesque channel, with boats passing each other in opposite directions – powerboats, sailboats, tugs and fishing vessels. Across the water, on the other side, an inviting village hugs the shore. "Now this is more like it," Robert says. "This is wonderful." Then he catches himself. "Sorry, I slipped into vacation mode there."

"We'll swing into town and look around," Shane says. "I don't know what we're looking for but we'll know it when we see it, I guess. We need some lunch anyway."

Shane parks on the waterfront and they walk two blocks to the town café, eyeballing the procession of motor homes, high-end SUVs and other vehicles lined up on the congested street. No trucks on this street even remotely fit the description of the one they're looking for. At the café a handful of customers, mostly locals it appears, hold forth at tables around the room. They choose a spot near the back, fairly private, where they can talk.

The waitress arrives with menus. "You boys here on business?" she asks.

"You could put it that way," Shane says.

"Yeah," she says. "Cause you don't look like farmers and you don't look like tourists."

"Are you cops?" a voice asks from behind them. Shane turns to find a heavyset old guy coming out of the restroom. He's wearing the black uniform of a town police officer.

"Are we that obvious?" Robert asks, pulling aside his shirt to reveal his trooper badge clipped to his belt.

"It's either that or you're professional hit-men. It's the outline of your shoulder harnesses under your shirts," the LaConner cop says. "And it's a warm day; you're overdressed." The officer puts his hand on the back of a third chair at the table. "Do you mind?" he asks, pulling out the chair with a loud scrape and sitting down hard. The three men introduce themselves to one another.

"Idaho?" the cop remarks when Robert introduces himself. "You're a long way from home."

"Well it was Alaska before that. Shane and I are old friends from another case."

The cop sighs. "Ok, that explains the Eskimo thing."

Robert scowls.

"Oh, I'm sorry," the officer says. "Samoan."

"Inuit," Robert clarifies.

"You could pass for Swinomish. You must be part of the manhunt for that guy who killed the cop the other day."

"That's right," Shane says.

"So what brings you over this way?"

"Following a hunch," Robert says, distracted by the menu. "Grasping at straws."

The waitress arrives and takes their orders – burgers for each of them. "I can't do this when Marie's around," Robert confesses. Nobody speaks for a moment.

"Anything going on here that's caught your eye lately?" Shane asks.

"This is a tourist town," the cop says. "Not much happens here. People come here to eat salmon, get an ice cream cone, buy things they don't need and look at the boats."

Shane explains the thinking behind their decision to come this way today. He and Robert believe that if the fugitive in the truck is headed for Seattle, he'll take the back roads through the reservation and LaConner, across Fir Island and on to Stanwood and Silvana. So they're driving his route, hoping to get lucky. "We figure he does his driving at night and hunkers down in the daytime."

"Well that's interesting," the cop says.

Robert asks him some questions about the town and its history, and the reservation. The cop patiently answers all his questions, then wants to ask a couple more of his own.

"You said this guy is driving a truck."

"That's right."

"Can you describe him?"

Robert gives him the outline.

"Well . . ." the cop says, "there was something earlier. I was doing a vehicle check at the park – noticed a Home Depot truck sitting there as if it had been parked all night. We don't allow that. The driver came walking up while I was looking at it. Apologized. Said he'd walked to town and back on the trail under the bridge."

Shane pushes back his chair and stands.

"How long ago?"

"Two hours maybe. I didn't care for the guy."

"Why's that?"

"Well for one thing he went out of his way to badmouth the

157

tribe. Said it was a shame our pretty town had to look at the reservation."

"Thanks for your help," Shane says, pulling his wallet from his back pocket and putting cash on the table. He and Robert head out the door. Shane remembers something and turns back to the cop.

"Hey," Shane calls. "Was this guy alone?"

"That's right – alone. Why do you ask?"

"Just curious."

"I hope you catch him," the cop calls behind them.

*

"Still no sign of his partner," Shane says as he and Robert hurry to the car. "What the heck are they up to?"

"I think he's a lone wolf at this point," Robert says as Shane hits the door-release button on his key fob.

"Call my office," Shane asks him as they pile into his car, "and let them know we're pretty sure we've picked up Cobb's trail. Tell them we believe the truck is headed for the federal courthouse in Seattle and that it says Home Depot now." They buckle their seat belts. "After you do that, call the inn and tell Brad that it looks like his theory was right."

Robert makes the calls as Shane drives them east past dairy herds, tulip fields, farm stands and croplands, then south along Pleasant Ridge. To the east, the view for miles is of a wide, flat agricultural valley. Moments later they cross a bridge over the North Fork of the Skagit River. Shane explains they're now on the delta. Robert looks to his left for a stunning view of a snow covered peak.

"Mt. Baker," Shane says.

They pass a sandwich board for immodest ice cream cones that would sound good to Shane on any other day – if the circumstances were different.

"This is his route," Shane says. "I guarantee you it is. I don't know where he'll stop, so we need to try to think like a guy who doesn't want to be seen. Since he's on the move because the cop disturbed him, my guess is that he'll try to get closer to Seattle before holing up for the night."

They pass an historic old white church and leave the delta as they cross the river's south fork. At the next intersection, the little community of Conway, Shane turns right and continues toward Stanwood on the old, two-lane, north-south highway. At Stanwood they do a quick drive-through of town, see no sign of a truck, and continue south on the back roads toward Silvana.

"There are a lot of places out here to hide a truck," Robert remarks.

"It'll be a miracle if we find him," Shane says. "But there's a Home Depot this side of Marysville and we should swing through that parking lot for sure." What he doesn't mention is that there's also a big Wal-Mart, Costco, Outlet Mall and sprawling commercial development. It's a far cry from laid-back Whidbey Island. They're truly looking for a needle in a haystack over here.

"If he's headed for Seattle's federal courthouse," Robert asks, "realistically, when do you think is the earliest he'll attempt to bomb it?"

"Tomorrow morning," Shane says. "Given where he was this morning. I think he'll probably want to lay over one more night en route so he can get into position to act in the morning."

"Except that so many eyes are watching that courthouse now, I don't see any way he can possibly hope to get close," Robert points out.

*

Cobb merges onto Interstate 5 southbound at the Arlington interchange. He hates the freeway. No sooner does he get up to speed than he passes a state patrol vehicle on the shoulder, red and blue lights flashing. The officer stands at the driver's-side window of a car he has stopped, examining license and registration, Cobb assumes.

Cobb watches in his mirror as the officer continues to look down at the items in his hand. The officer makes no move toward his car but Cobb cannot take a chance. Just ahead he takes the next exit into a highway rest stop and parks in the truck area, between two eighteen-wheelers. He'll cool his heels here. He sits in the cab to think.

Moments later the same state patrol vehicle pulls into the rest area on the other side and parks. The officer gets out, cinches up his belt, puts on his cap and walks toward the restroom. The second he disappears inside, Cobb starts his engine and pulls out, accelerating onto the freeway again.

This was just coincidence, he thinks – bad luck but also good luck because this officer had other things on his mind. But that nosy cop in LaConner was different. In hindsight, Cobb wishes he had ushered him to the Happy Hunting Ground. He almost followed him into the restroom. He sat in the cab for a moment with the engine idling and weighed the tradeoffs. He couldn't afford another dead cop to call attention to himself. But on the other hand, he left a loose end that could come back to haunt him.

Suddenly, in Cobb's side mirror, he sees flashing red and blue lights – at least three sets. This is it. They're gaining on him fast and he decelerates toward the shoulder, reaching under his jacket on the passenger seat for his handgun. But the lead car, a state patrol SUV, shoots past him doing ninety mph and keeps going. Cobb is shaking now and he's astonished. Two Snohomish County Sheriff's vehicles follow the patrol vehicle. He watches them weave across three lanes of traffic as startled motorists pull to the right shoulder but can't get there fast enough.

Moments later, Cobb passes all three of the police vehicles stopped in front, beside and behind a Home Depot box truck on the shoulder. Officers with guns drawn use the open doors of their vehicles as shields, standing behind them and crouching as two other officers approach the truck. No one even looks up as he passes.

But my god, they know they're looking for a Home Depot truck. He's got to get off this highway right now; the search is red hot.

How did they figure it out so fast? Then it hits him – the LaConner cop, the loose end he almost went back and cleaned up.

Cobb sees an exit for Costco ahead. It seems a good place to get lost in a sea of vehicles, and he pulls off the freeway. Besides, this exit offers a choice of restaurants for his last meal. Increasingly, he suspects, that's how this is going to end.

*

At the inn, Brad sits on the porch with a book about the history of socialist colonies in Washington and struggles to keep his eyes open. These lazy summer afternoons work their spell on a guy, but his thoughts keep drifting to Robert and Shane.

Marie comes up the lane from the mailbox with a copy of *The Seattle Times* and tosses it into the chair beside him as she walks inside. Maybe the newspaper will perk him up. He picks it up and opens it, but his mind is elsewhere.

Robert's call a while ago was encouraging. Robert and Shane are hard on the trail of their man – maybe just two hours behind. But Brad can't stop puzzling over the intended target. Seattle's Federal Building is such an obvious target that security will be impossibly high, especially after Robert found the discarded photo at the safe house. Why would Cobb even consider an attack where he couldn't possibly succeed?

Brad focuses on the newspaper. The news is predictable. Boeing tests a new version of its workhorse 737. The president tweets new threats to shut down the government if he doesn't get a border wall. Republican leaders wish he would stop tweeting. More than a hundred extra agents of the FBI and Bureau of Alcohol Tobacco and Firearms (ATF) converge on north Puget Sound to hunt for a domestic terrorist believed planning a bomb attack. Seattle is preparing for a large civil rights march tomorrow.

Wherever those agents are headquartered, the testosterone must be off the charts. Maybe the testosterone is what it takes to go to work every day knowing you might not come home.

Nothing seemed this complicated when Brad was younger. People like Robert and Shane, and Marie and Elizabeth, and their children will have to live in this new world of intolerance and suspicion if things don't turn around soon. Maybe the younger generation can fix it. He hopes so.

Irene, Elizabeth, Billy and Judy emerge from the garden, fanning the air with their sketchbooks to dry the watercolors they've applied to their sketches. "Time to start some dinner," Elizabeth says. "A little wine makes the hours fly."

"Let me see what you've got," Brad asks Billy, standing up for a closer look. It's a sketch of Moose on a patch of lush grass. The white Bichon Frise on green grass is bold and striking. "That is good," Brad says. "Really good. You even captured his expression and his pink tongue."

"Don't you think he has talent?" Judy asks.

"He's a smart kid," Brad says. "Fast learner."

Judy smiles. "This is the most quality time I've had with Billy in ages, just sketching, relaxing and hanging out with this group. It feels good – really settled." With Cobb and Franks both still at large, Shane has insisted she stay at the inn for her own safety.

Brad follows the group up the steps and into the parlor, where he sits down at his laptop and powers up. He lays out the newspaper beside him on the table. After finding the article about the march a few minutes ago, there's something he wants to check.

Brad scrolls over the streets of Seattle on Google Earth. From time to time he refers to the map in *The Seattle Times* showing the route of tomorrow's civil rights march through the city, which starts on Capitol Hill and continues for a mile, ending at Westlake Center downtown. Seattle Police will be stretched thin with crowd control, intersection closures and basic security over such an extended route.

Opposition groups have not announced any plans to put counter-protesters at the march, though it's likely that some "Make America Great" people will show. Sadly, Brad thinks, equal opportunity and equal rights are not the kind of greatness they want to go back to.

In addition to parishioners from several large black churches in the city, the parade will also draw participation from gay pride groups, feminist organizations, the Seattle Men's Choir, marching bands from Seattle's predominantly black Central District, abortion rights activists, Planned Parenthood, the Islamic community, American Indian Movement, the local homeless coalition and an alphabet soup of other advocacy groups.

It will surely be a hectic day for police, he thinks. If this weren't enough, they must also maintain tighter-than-usual surveillance of the Federal Building and its approaches in light that a truck bomber may be headed there.

*

Shane exits onto Quil Ceda Boulevard on the outskirts of Marysville and heads for the Wal-Mart Super Center. "I admit I'm stumped," he declares. "I don't know what else to do but cruise these big parking lots in case he decides to overnight in one of them. This is as good as anyplace. Wal-Mart is pretty lenient about overnighters. I really don't think he's heading into the city at the end of the day."

They check the entire lot, then head for Home Depot on this same commercial strip. Here, they find several trucks with the Home Depot logo but none that come close in size and description to the one Cobb's driving.

"Now what?" Robert asks.

"What do you think?" Shane replies. "We're not really getting anywhere. Do you want to go home?"

"We've come this far. I don't mind staying the night. I think he's around here someplace and I don't want to go home till we see it through, one way or the other."

"Then let's look around the reservation some more. This whole area is Tulalip Reservation land, under the jurisdiction of tribal police." He calls the tribal police headquarters and informs them he's tracking a suspect in a box truck who may be in the area, and that he'll be looking around on reservation roads. They thank him for the courtesy.

Shane heads back to the frontage road and begins a systematic search of reservation roads, focusing on congested areas where a truck could blend into the confusion. He's just passing the tribal police headquarters and a large car dealership when Robert's cell phone rings.

"It's Brad," Robert announces. "He wants to know our plans for the evening." Robert fills him in. They're tired and frustrated but sticking with it. "We'll get a hotel," Robert says, "and get back at it first thing tomorrow. We're just wrapping up here for today."

Shane pulls over so Elizabeth can talk with him for a moment. Then she gives the phone to Marie. Shane gives Robert's phone back to Robert so he can say goodnight to her. After Marie finishes, it turns out Brad wants to talk to Robert again, so he hands the phone back to Brad.

"This is crazy," Robert says. "There must be an easier way for us all to talk."

"I just wanted to ask," Brad begins, "if you know where the ATF and FBI are staying. I saw in the paper they've flooded the area with about 100 extra agents."

Robert asks Shane.

"No idea," Shane says.

"Well it might be something to check," Brad says. "Seattle is going to be a complete mess tomorrow with the big civil rights march. You may find it hard to move around."

Shane files the question with a hundred others floating around in his mind. He wonders if Cobb had this all figured out when he planned his attack or whether he just got lucky. Either way, he's got the law enforcement community tied up in knots.

*

"Here's the answer to Brad's question about the feds," Shane declares as he and Robert enter the casino's high-rise hotel and head for the reception desk. The lobby is crawling with single men in bulky sport coats that don't seem to fit over their torsos very well.

"Do you need a hand with luggage?" a hotel employee asks.

"Actually no," Robert says. "What you see is what you get."

"Oh you're with the group," the bellhop says.

"Apparently," Robert remarks.

Robert and Shane head directly for the restaurant and bar, passing a closed conference room on the way with a door card that says "Task Force."

At the restaurant they notice several men in earnest conversation standing by the bar in a wide stance, some with arms folded, others with one hand on a hip and the other wrapped around a drink with ice. They project a certain swagger even when standing still, and occupy every table and barstool.

"Let's come back in a few minutes," Shane says.

"What, and miss a chance to do some networking?"

"Spare me."

The elevator is smooth and fast. They walk down a short corridor, past a linen cart and a maid who smiles. They swipe Shane's magnetic card in the lock, which buzzes to let them in. The room is airy and pleasant. Shane crosses to the window and opens the floor-to-ceiling drapes, and looks down seven stories at the loading dock. Not much to see on the back side of the building but this room is a little less expensive than the ones on the other side with the better view.

Turning away from the windows, he declares, "I think the buffet is still open. We can get some inexpensive dinner there and steer clear of the macho group at the restaurant and bar."

An hour later, after a leisurely trip through the line and two heaping plates of roast beef, salmon and new potatoes, they ride the elevator back to their floor.

The stress of the day is beginning to wear off now, and both men are feeling drowsy. Within half an hour they struggle to keep their eyes open. It's the big dinner making them sleepy, Shane thinks. They turn out the light, planning to get up early in the morning and head directly for downtown Seattle before rush hour. It promises to be an eventful day. They'll either stop Ray Cobb from what he intends to do or have a front row seat for it.

Sleep comes fitfully; Shane tosses and turns. The civil rights march downtown tomorrow really throws a wrench into things. Traffic and parking will be impossible. The police will be spread thin, pulled away from the Federal Building to watch a sprawling parade route. It crosses Shane's mind that Cobb might have planned for this all along – either to dilute police presence at the Federal Building or to hit the parade instead. Shane and Robert's job just got exponentially harder.

The numerals on the bedside clock read 2:36 a.m. when Shane decides he'll never get back to sleep again if he doesn't use the bathroom. Not to disturb Robert, who is snoring lightly, Shane crosses the room in the dark. On his way back to bed a moment later, groggy and only half awake, he pauses to look out the window at the deceptively peaceful night.

If he could see into the distance, he'd be looking right at Whidbey Island. The world is asleep. Somewhere just over the horizon are Elizabeth, Billy and Judy. He never dreamed they'd ever be under the same roof even temporarily, but life throws surprises at us that no one can predict.

In a few hours he's pretty sure something terrible is going to happen. The odds that he and Robert can prevent it seem impossibly long but they have to try. His brain struggles to imagine how different this peaceful day will be if Raymond Cobb succeeds in his plan.

The view takes a moment to register.

"Oh shit!" Shane yells, flipping on the lights. "Get up! We've got to get out of here right now. Hit the fire alarm," he yells to Robert as he reaches for his gun and his pants, tripping over himself as he puts one leg into them and opens the door. "Grab your gun. Take the stairs," he yells.

Seven stories directly below the room, a Home Depot box truck sits right next to the building, by the loading dock. A solitary figure walks away from it toward the woods, carrying something long.

Chapter 19

Shane and Robert race down the stairs to the basement and through the hotel's busy kitchen and laundry with their guns drawn. A dozen startled hotel employees dive for the floor. "Police!" Shane yells. "Get away from the building. There's a bomb." Employees scream, get up and run for the doors.

Shane and Robert try several unmarked doors before finding the right one with a release bar to the outside. "Stay away from the truck," Shane yells to the crowd behind him as he runs right toward it.

Cobb has disappeared into the night but there's only one place he can be – in the woods across from the hotel with a clear line of fire at the truck. The long object he was carrying looked to Shane like a grenade launcher or high-powered rifle. They may have only seconds to stop him. Shane hopes hotel guests took the fire alarm seriously and are pouring into the parking lot on the lobby side. The building must hold hundreds of casino guests in addition to the large contingent of FBI and ATF. In hindsight, he thinks, Cobb's plan was brilliant.

The night is dark but the lights of the casino complex are better than nothing – it's all they've got.

Shane scans the woods. Suddenly, a short distance away, a bright flame illuminates Cobb's face as he flicks his lighter for one last cigarette. "There!" he yells to Robert, pointing. He and Robert empty their clips at the spot and brace for what they fear is coming next.

But the night is suddenly silent. Shane listens for an explosion but it does not come.

They approach the spot cautiously, still holding their guns in the two-handed firing position. Cobb lies crumpled face down on the ground, bleeding from an artery wound in the leg. Blood also oozes from several other wounds in his chest and abdomen. The back of his head is gone. He's lying on top of the grenade launcher.

Shane kneels down by the suspect and feels for a pulse in the carotid artery, though it's gratuitous with the head wound. "He's finished," Shane declares as several FBI and ATF agents come running toward them.

Shane turns to the officers behind him. "The truck is a bomb," pointing back toward the hotel. "This grenade launcher was the detonator – I think. We need to get the truck away from there ASAP." He rolls Cobb over, patting his pockets, feeling for the keys. When he finds them he digs them out and hands them to one of the agents.

"I'm still shaking," the agent says. "That was as close as it gets."

"We got lucky," Shane replies.

Sirens, horns and flashing lights fill the night. Police and fire engines surround the hotel. Firemen with oxygen tanks on their backs rush into the lobby. Men in underwear talk in small groups. Guests in nightclothes mill around in the parking lot.

"It's going to take a while to sort this out," Shane says.

*

Laughter fills the room as Shane and Elizabeth's guests sit round the table watching Billy open his presents. Brad's eyes go from face to face, studying the smiles. Elizabeth and Judy sit on either side of Billy, cheering him on and piling the wrappings out of the way. Irene squeezes Brad's hand under the table and winks.

At Robert's signal, the room goes dark and Marie enters dramatically, carrying a cake with twelve flaming candles. She sets it in front of Billy, who closes his eyes briefly to concentrate on his wish. Then he blows out the candles and the room lights come up. Everyone claps and cheers. The cake, topped with Marie's artificial rocks, is a masterpiece.

"What did you wish for?" Irene asks.

"That both of my moms and all my friends will be together for my birthday again next year."

Things worked out well, but two children at this table nearly lost their fathers. Brad knows that Elizabeth and Marie are thinking about that. As it turned out, Robert and Shane denied the supremacist movement a hero. This vacation was everything Brad dreamed it would be, notwithstanding that. He confessed his secret and it didn't ruin anything. Now he can go home and take care of that unfinished business with his Chinese friend, "Boise." Brad thinks he's ready now.

Robert turns to Brad. "Shane told me what you're facing when you get back."

"Oh that. Just one of those projects in life that has to be done. If all goes well it'll be a few months of inconvenience and nothing more."

"Well," Robert says, "just know that we're right there in Boise and you have a place to stay with us as often as you need it. We're going to keep a close eye on what happens and we'll be there for you. I think you know that."

"I do."

Ironically, despite the good outcome of the hunt for Cobb, Brad knows Shane is troubled by some unfinished business of his own. Shane and Robert stopped the bombing and saved hundreds of lives, but had to kill the only witness who could tell them where Fred Franks might be. Franks is now wanted on a federal warrant for conspiracy to commit a terrorist act against the United States. Police in all fifty states will be looking for him. Jerry Buckley is behind bars and likely to stay there. Franks must be long gone.

Then there's Shane's ex-wife, Judy. By her own grit she saved herself from captivity and possible death. Perhaps they all underestimated her. Lord knows she has her flaws, Brad thinks, though no more than his own. By surviving and escaping, she earned a new measure of respect from Shane and an outpouring of gratitude and kindness from the group. Judy finally belongs, Brad thinks. She has found her community and it is them – all of them here in this room.

*

Early the next morning, while the others sleep, Shane slips out of bed in the darkness. He grabs his clothes and heads for the bathroom to dress, then continues down the hall toward the kitchen. He is just reaching for the front door when Marie catches him.

"Sneaking out?" she asks.

"Going for a drive." He explains that he wants to take one more look at the safe house where Cobb and Franks holed up for several days.

"Want some company?"

"Sure. I can always use fresh eyes."

"I'll leave Robert a note. Promise me we'll stop somewhere for coffee." Marie finds a scratch pad by the phone and composes a note to Robert and the rest of the group.

They head down the driveway and Shane turns toward Freeland. They ride in silence for a moment, then Shane begins, "I've been so preoccupied I don't think I've asked you how it feels to be a mother."

Marie replies that it's an adjustment – a big one after years of building her career as a single woman in what's still mostly a man's world, wildlife enforcement. But marriage and motherhood feel right to her. "I'm truly happy," she says. "I love Martin and Robert, and Robert is the best partner a woman could ever hope to find."

"You don't miss the excitement of the job a little?"

Marie hesitates.

"No." Then, a few seconds later, "Yes."

"The truth is I do," she admits. "I loved trespassing into the Buckley compound with Robert. It was like old times. In a few years when Martin is older I think I can get back to my career."

Shane nods. "It's an addiction," he says, "for me anyway. I love catching bad guys. I'm scared silly my addiction will come between Elizabeth and me, like it did with Judy. I don't want that to happen."

"Elizabeth isn't Judy. She's solid as a rock and I don't think it will."

"So you don't think I should worry?"

"Elizabeth loves the life you've made together. She knew what she was signing up for when she married you."

"I hope you're right," Shane says.

"Just don't take her for granted and you two will be fine."

"Robert told me he has applied for a job as the governor's driver."

"Yes, I'm excited for him. The two of them really hit it off. It's a promotion and a great assignment, and it should keep him out of harm's way."

"I hear you."

"The governor may find it hard to do any work in the car because the two of them talk about Alaska all the time. When the governor was in college, I guess he worked on a fish processing barge in Dutch Harbor."

"Has he met you yet?"

"Not yet."

"I think that will seal the deal."

They both laugh.

They stop at the phone company's café and get their coffee drinks, then sip them as they drive north, making small talk about the birthday party and the wonderful time everyone had on this vacation, notwithstanding the stress of the chase that consumed Shane. Marie says the change she's seen in Judy during her stay at the lodge is heartening.

Shane nods.

"This case is still bothering you, isn't it?" Marie asks. Shane admits that it is. The part he could never reconcile is why Franks disappeared and left Cobb to carry out the plot alone.

"Did Franks change his mind?" Marie asks.

"It's possible. But guys like that, veterans of the movement, don't usually walk away till they've done what they came to do. I wish we could have asked Cobb some questions, but it didn't work out that way."

Shane turns up the narrow lane to the clearing and barn in the woods where Cobb and Franks hid out for several days. "I keep wondering if I missed something," he says. "I've gone over and over it in my mind. This is the last place we know they were together. Robert and I came back and re-searched this site after Jerry first told us about it."

At the barn Shane parks and they both get out. The summer morning air is pleasant. The cows in the pasture come over to moo at them. Violet-green Swallows dive and swoop for insects over the field. Shane opens the barn door and they step inside. Chickens come running to see if they're being fed.

"Who normally takes care of this place and the animals?" Marie asks.

"I guess it used to be Jerry, but now I suppose his folks will swing by once in a while."

"You aren't going to prosecute them?"

"No I don't think so. This plot wasn't their idea. They're old and basically finished. Jerry is behind bars, and he represented the future. I look for the compound to fade away now."

Shane and Marie walk around, prodding at the hay with their feet, looking for evidence – shell casings or cigarette butts, half-eaten sandwiches, blood, anything that might tell a story. Against a wall Shane notices an assortment of tools – shovels, axes and saws, as one would expect in an old barn like this.

They spend several minutes carefully inspecting the barn. "I'm getting nothing," Marie says, stepping outside into the sunshine and looking up at the blue sky.

Shane follows her, closes the door behind them, and stands silently for a moment, looking out across the clearing at the woods in the distance.

"I sometimes think," Shane says, "that if I just stand in a place long enough, I will begin to feel something – get a picture of what happened. But then other times I think that's crazy."

"I don't think it's crazy," Marie replies. She watches a coyote on the far side of the clearing, sticking to the shadows, slinking in and out of the trees. "We have a sixth sense, I think, that we don't use very much. It's present in all of us but not well developed."

"You think so?" Shane asks.

"We're primates; it's part of our makeup, buried in our DNA. That coyote is using it," Marie says, pointing across the clearing. "I fell back on intuition in some of my poaching cases when I was miles from nowhere in the wilderness, all alone, with no distractions."

They stand together for a moment in silence, alone with their thoughts. Then Marie adds, "You see the sixth sense in animals all the time. But in animals it's way more developed. They know things in a different way than we do."

"I think that's why you were good at your job," Shane says. "You were in tune with nature – with the animals."

"That coyote felt our presence," she remarks, "knew we were here before it saw us. At the same time it's curious about something in the field that's worth taking the risk to reveal itself to us. Don't you wish you could know what that coyote knows?" Marie asks.

"Yeah, if it could tell me where Fred Franks is," Shane laughs.

She and Shane watch as the coyote stops and sniffs at the ground, walks around a spot and paws at it a little, then looks up. It stands and stares directly at Shane and Marie for a long minute, its two pointed ears perfectly framed against the green background. Then it trots away, into the brush.

"Probably stalking a rabbit," Shane says.

Afterword

On December 7, 1984, some 100 heavily armed federal agents, assisted by local law enforcement, the U.S. Coast Guard and a helicopter, sealed off Whidbey Island. Agents crawled through the woods of Central Whidbey neighborhoods to surround houses occupied by members of a neo-Nazi splinter group, The Order, who had taken refuge in the Greenbank area.

The Coast Guard closed the main north-south shipping lane between the island and the Olympic Peninsula. They arrested several members of the organization and cornered its leader, Robert Mathews, in a cabin on Smugglers Cove Road, where a pitched battle raged for 24 hours. Mathews died when the cabin burned to the ground after an illumination flare set it on fire.

The Order's crime spree included the murder of Denver talk radio host Alan Berg, the $3 million robbery of a Brinks armored car in northern California, firing at FBI agents in Idaho, counterfeiting US currency, and wounding an FBI agent in Portland, Oregon.

Mathews had read and been inspired by the neo-Nazi novel, *The Turner Diaries,* and his group was using it as a blueprint for action. He and other group members also had spent time at the 20-acre compound of The Aryan Nations in Hayden Lake, Idaho, headquarters of Rev. Richard Butler's supremacist Church of Jesus Christ Christian.

Compiled from multiple sources including *The Seattle Times, The Washington Post, Whidbey-News Times, UPI Archives.*

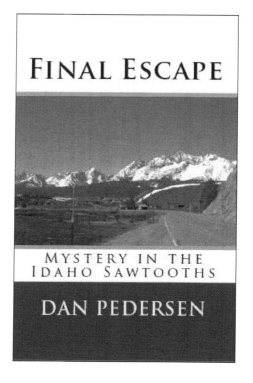

From *Final Escape:*
Mystery in the Idaho Sawtooths
Book 3 in this Series
Available from Amazon.com and Whidbey Island bookstores

On the porch after dinner, Brad breaks out two Mt. Borah
Brown Ales for Shane and himself while Elizabeth and Irene clink
glasses of wine. Brad notices Elizabeth looks especially beautiful in
the soft light of the early evening, her long red hair catching the sun.
Did she fix herself up a little extra? He catches Shane's eyes lingering
on her.

In the distance, the soulful melody of a harmonica floats their
way on the breeze.

"That's Bolivar," Brad says, "introducing Billy to the
harmonica. He's not bad, don't you think?"

Brad explains to Shane that the ale comes from a small craft brewery in Salmon, several hours north. "I think it's a delicious beer and it brings back memories of the time I climbed Mt. Borah in the Air Force."

"You were 20-something?" Shane asks.

"Yeah. About that."

"Reliving past glories," Shane laughs.

"Exactly."

Irene interjects. "He has a rich fantasy life."

Brad stares at her with a knowing smile. "I happen to like my fantasies," and then back at Shane. "Seriously, Shane, while Billy is with Bolivar and we have a few minutes, I wanted to ask your advice about a problem Elizabeth is having."

Shane leans forward and listens while Brad outlines the situation. When he finishes, Shane leans back and turns to Elizabeth, "Is it the same guy?"

"I don't think so."

"Because of the black hair? The pony tail?"

"Mainly that."

"I think it might be him," he says. "Otherwise it's an awfully big coincidence. It wouldn't be a hard disguise."

Brad adds, "There's something else. I didn't mention this to Elizabeth earlier, but we've started getting some harassing phone messages and hang-ups here at the ranch."

"What are the messages?"

"To keep our noses out of other people's business."

"Interesting! Well that takes it to another level."

"You think it's connected to me?" Elizabeth asks.

"I think there's a good chance. It all fits the pattern of a stalker who's obsessed with you and trying to make sure you can't have a life without him."

"Oh god," she moans. "This is bad."

"Not at all," Shane says. "We can handle this. I hate these creeps. They're predators and parasites, and push people around, but at heart they're pathetic and weak."

"But how would he even know about Brad and Irene?"

"He was in your house, wasn't he?" Shane asks. "Did he see your mail? Did he get into your computer?"

"Well he saw everything else."

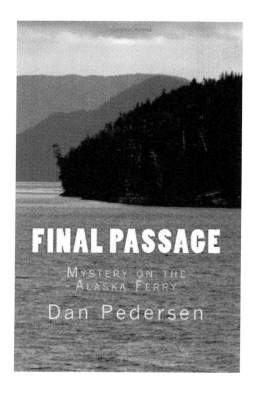

From *Final Passage:*
An Alaska Ferry Mystery
Book 2 in this Series
Available from Amazon.com and Whidbey Island bookstores

The Matanuska inches ahead between flashing navigation buoys in Wrangell Narrows, changing course at each marker to stay within this twisting channel. Evening is falling and a campfire burns brightly on shore a hundred yards away. Sweet smoke from the fire drifts over the ship and takes Brad back to times he and Irene spent in the mountains of Idaho with their friends of a lifetime, Stu and Amy, both now gone. It's a bittersweet memory.

Brad imagines a family around that campfire, roasting weenies and marshmallows, or maybe good friends talking about their day. Smoke drifts toward the ferry from woodstoves in cozy cabins so close they could shout to the owners. A dog barks. A couple standing on their deck wave to the ship and Brad waves back.

*

Petersburg is a storybook scene on this quiet night. Irene is glad she made the effort to stay up. The lights of the town and its many boats must hold a thousand secrets of ordinary people and their Alaska-size dreams on the edge of the civilized world.

Moonlight bathes the snowfields of nearby peaks. This is the prettiest place she has seen on this trip, a pocket of humanity in the heart of wilderness, surrounded by water, mountains, glaciers and forest. She has this moment to herself, the other passengers having retired to their cabins for the evening. She lingers a while, then starts a leisurely circuit around the deck, taking in the view and the aromas of creosoted pilings, fish canneries, fir trees . . .

The impact from behind knocks the wind from Irene's lungs and sends her reeling forward, fighting for balance. She grabs wildly for the rail with her right arm and barely catches it, staying half on her feet, unable to breathe. Her heart pounds and her legs fold. She wraps her body over the rail and gasps in shock, staring down at the white bubbles where the bow slices through the blackness. Half a minute passes with no air. She's in full panic.

Then, ever so slowly, her diaphragm responds and her lungs draw air. She straightens up and wonders what happened. She is alone on the deck – no passengers, no crew. The ship already is in open water, accelerating toward Juneau.

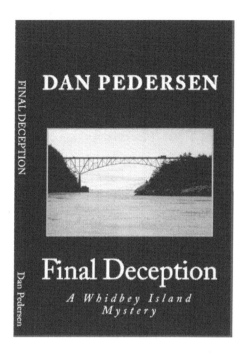

From *Final Deception:*
A Whidbey Island Mystery
Book 1 in This Series
Available from Amazon.com and Whidbey Island bookstores

In the blackness, Bella Morelli pitched face forward in an
ungainly dive, wind roaring in her ears. The four seconds took
forever and she had two last thoughts – surprise and dread. She hit
the water all wrong like a breaching whale, lungs first, a horrible
impact, and that was the last she felt.

*

Deception Pass Bridge connects Washington's Fidalgo and
Whidbey islands across a deep chasm. It is 180 feet from the bridge
deck to the water, depending on tide. From there it's 130 more in icy
darkness to the bottom.

A young person in peak condition, hitting the water feet first in perfect form, can survive if they miss the rocks and regain the surface before drowning or hypothermia. A 67-year-old cannot. Whirlpools and eddies reach out to clutch and pull them down.

*

Decades ago Brad had almost cracked the mystery of Bella. She had taken a road trip with him, taken a risk. Brad registered them in a Tennessee motel as Mr. and Mrs. Brad Haraldsen.

They hadn't discussed the sleeping arrangement – it just happened. They were two unmarried 25-year-olds traveling in the South in 1972. Gatlinburg was a honeymoon destination and the couple's eyes glistened with new love. Even in civilian attire, Brad carried himself with military bearing. That and his clean-cut, neatly trimmed hair were assets in the South where patriotism ran high.

As it was, the clerk didn't question their marital status – gave them a room by the pool in the nearly vacant auto court.

A heavy sky threatened afternoon lightning. Brad and Bella swam anyway and washed the miles from the road. Then, five years into their friendship, they made love for the first time as comfortably as if it were every day.

The lovemaking was slow and satisfying, their private secret as the storm rumbled through the lush hills beyond the thick curtains. Afterwards, they lay in each other's arms. Bella smiled and Brad felt her caution about him wash away.

A lifetime later, sitting on his mountain in Stanley, Idaho, Brad still teared up at the memory, as vivid now as it had ever been. That time, that place to which they had never returned, was the happiest of his life. Brad's eyes stung and he closed them to see it all again. He remembered every detail of that motel, that room, the long journey that led there.

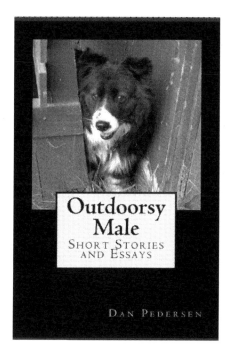

From *Outdoorsy Male:*
Short Stories and Essays
Available from Amazon.com and Whidbey Island bookstores

Don't Photograph My Wattles

"I have only one vice," my old kindergarten classmate announces as she fishes a pack of American Spirit cigarettes from her bag and lights one.

A blue cloud engulfs us as we huddle under an awning in a chilly October-morning rain. Tammi has just finished a sesame bagel with cream cheese at the Bakery by the Sea in the quaint village of Langley, Whidbey Island.

"Well that sure was disappointing," she declares, screwing up her face.

"The bagel?"

"Yeah. Not that good."

"I sneak a glance at my watch because we are already late to the workshop she is presenting this morning."

"You say this is the only bakery in this backwater?" She asks.
"Only one."
"Crap."
Nodding at the cigarette pack in her yellow fingers, the points out, "At least they're all natural." She smiles for the first time this morning. "No artificial additives. No genetically modified tobacco."
Then she adds, "You can stop looking at your watch because I'm not going to rush this."
The smoke, which clings to us like burning tires, saturates my blue jacket and gray beard.
We are getting reacquainted after Tammi's first night in my garage guest apartment. I haven't seen her for about 60 years. She asks for a wakeup call, which I place to her iPhone at the stroke of 7:45.
"Yeah, I'm up," she answers with a voice like gravel, then apparently goes down again.
It turns out Tammi doesn't like the fruit and one-minute oatmeal I've stocked for her in the Guest Apartment by the Sea, nor the coffee. "I'm not an oatmeal fan, she says. "And to be honest I just didn't feel like cooking breakfast this morning." So at the last second she asks if I will drive her someplace for a bagel.
"I don't do dairy, sugar or wheat," she declares. "Or GMO."
As an afterthought she adds, "You only get one body."
I am struggling with every part of this.
Standing in the weather, she fills in a piece of her story. "My life is the shits. I know the reason I'm not wearing a ring on this finger is because I'm a nag. Well, that and some other things. That alcoholic turd I married wasted my best years. I've got nothing to show for it now but a bad back, a mountain of debt and a pack of dogs. I have this fantasy I'm going to meet a nice man on Whidbey Island, marry him and live happily ever after."
She sucks another lungful of smoke and blows it all over me.
"God, I hate being poor," she says. "I have no backup. Why does everyone else lead a charmed life but me?"
"It's all luck and timing," I say.
"I hate my gut," she remarks. "I swear I'm going to lose this spare tire. I know you plan to take pictures at the workshop. Keep in mind, I don't photograph well. I wave my arms and that makes my wattles hop around. Do not photograph my wattles."

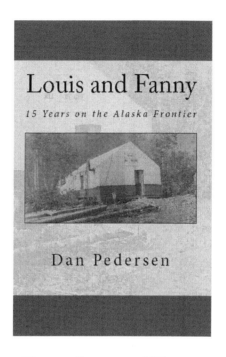

From *Louis and Fanny:*
15 Years on the Alaska Frontier
Available from Amazon.com and Whidbey Island bookstores

Trees sagged under a blanket of white. Boots kicked up powder in the streets of Seward, Alaska, as the mail steamer *Dora* pulled away from the dock. The ship trailed a plume of black smoke. Captain C.B. McMullen stood at the stern, taking a last look at civilization and pondering what he'd find on his return to Kodiak.

He'd just reached Seward with a firsthand account of conditions in the remote outpost of Kodiak. Mt. Katmai had exploded 100 miles from Kodiak in a volcanic eruption that was still spewing ash into the atmosphere. The *Dora* had called on Kodiak after tense hours sailing blind in conditions that could have cost McMullen the ship and all aboard.

Now he was going back with the minister's wife.

*

On Kodiak Island, ash filled the sky and blacked out the town for 60 hours. Landslides of ash swept away houses. People went hungry and expected to die. Lightning struck the Naval radio station, setting a fire and knocking out communication with the outside world. Ships' radios were useless with the electrical disturbance. Townspeople waited in darkness, their eyes and throats burning with dust, wondering if they could survive this, whatever it was.

Downwind, ash rained for a day at Juneau, across the Gulf of Alaska. In Vancouver, B.C., more than 1,000 miles from the volcano, people wondered if the sulfuric atmosphere was safe to breathe. It all happened just as the *Dora* was completing its westward run, bound for Kodiak a few hours ahead. It waited offshore till conditions cleared enough to approach Kodiak . . .

*

"The day was an exceptionally beautiful one and we were all on deck enjoying our cigar and the scenery when someone shouted: 'Look at the smoke.' Gazing off to the westward we beheld across Shelikof Straits, on the mainland, an immense column of smoke ascending skyward, its diameter seeming to be at least half a mile or a mile."

The volcano was 55 miles from their position, and Thwaites went on, "Of course we all thought of our cameras, but the distance was so great that the idea of securing a photograph was abandoned as impractical. We continued o watch the phenomenon when it began to dawn upon our minds that it was rapidly becoming dimmer, and that a dark mass of cloud was showing above the column, mingling with it and coming our way."

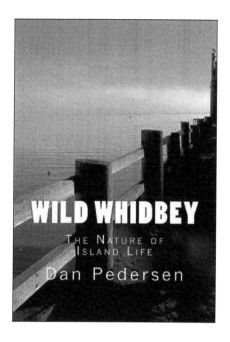

From Wild Whidbey:
The Nature of Island Life

In Full Color
Available from Amazon.com

People argue in circles about whether islands attract a certain kind of person or create them. I think it's both, but skewed toward the latter 30 years into my one-man study.

We make our big turns in life for complicated reasons, including luck and self-delusion. I had some romantic ideas about island life and they played a role in my irrational move to Whidbey Island when I still had a fulltime job in the city. I saw something wholesome here, wasn't sure how to explain it or get it, but hoped I'd figure it out . . .

The move was impulsive but soon became transformative . . . Waking up in a blissfully quiet place, I wasn't prepared for the birdsong. The woods act as a megaphone an hour before sunrise, when all the birds awaken with something to say. The songs change with the seasons and I started correlating the changes with seeing the first Rufous Hummingbirds of March, the first Violet-green Swallows, the first Black-headed Grosbeaks and Western Tanagers, even Great-horned Owls on foggy winter nights.

The spring migration is nature's timeless cycle. It's a barometer of how we are doing on this planet and takes place alongside but separate from our human concerns. To me it is comforting and reassuring amid the constant chaos of our world – war, crime and breaking news, politics, terrorism, jobs, divorce, drones, sickness, smart bombs and talk radio, and all the other noise that spews stress at us.

As time passed I started caring more about the cycles of nature than the cycles of news. In this I am well aware I am not normal or typical of most people and how they live . . .

I started counting the growth rings on the century-old tree rounds I was splitting, imagining the seasons those trees had seen. I found friends who cared about such details as much as I did. And I discovered the luxury of silence – the simple joys of a book and a camera, and some time outside.

Whidbey Island's abundant wildlife and forests, gentle people and creative community all claimed parts of my soul. All shaped my values and philosophy, and my temperament. I grew accustomed to kind smiles and cheery "good mornings" from both friends and strangers on the sidewalks of Langley and the trails in our woods. I stopped worrying about the person coming toward me in the dark.

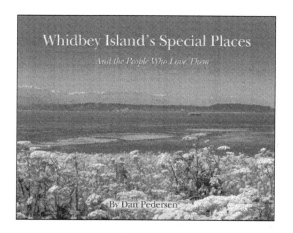

From Whidbey Island's Special Places
And the People Who Live There
Available from Whidbey Island bookstores

Standing in the shadows of giant old-growth firs and cedars at South Whidbey State Park, Elliott Menashe remembers a story. It's about a woman who attended one of his classes on forest management.

"She was imperious – a real tough cookie," he says, shaking his head. He'd been telling the class about forest snags and all the reasons to leave them intact as wildlife habitat, but the woman was not buying it. "I've got a 60-foot snag that's about six feet thick. "It's annoying me and I want it gone."

Menashe asked if it was a safety hazard. "No." And was it full of woodpecker holes?

"Yeah, it's got those. But I want it gone."

"You just moved here, right?" he asked, then offered her a deal. "Leave it alone, and in a year if you don't change your mind, I will pay for its removal."

About a year later a package showed up in Menashe's mail. "It's a bottle of really good wine. Chocolates. And pictures of, you know, baby owls, eagles, osprey, herons, kingfishers – all these pictures. She said, 'If you hadn't stopped me I would never have known what I was doing. Thank you so much. I look around me now with different eyes."

The story illustrates an error Menashe sees often as principal of Greenbelt Consulting, a natural resources consulting firm. Newcomers often don't seek advice about living in harmony with nature. Arriving on the island from an urban or suburban setting of traditional lawns and landscaping, and with little previous contact with wildlife and woodland processes, their first impulse is to clear a big view, eradicate native vegetation and replace it with neat, manicured suburbia.

In the process they destroy all the best, most wondrous and magical reasons to live on the island.

A good place to become immersed in those wonders is the mile-long Wilbert Trail, across Smuggler's Cove Road from the entrance to South Whidbey State Park. Parallel parking for several cars is available at the trailhead on a widened section of road shoulder about 0.4-mile north of the park entrance. It is marked with a crosswalk and a small sign identifying the Wilbert Trail.

"This is not a true old-growth forest," Menashe clarifies. "It's a mature forest with old-growth remnants." The distinction is important but takes nothing away from the impact. A few steps from the highway, hikers enter a sea of sword ferns. Several hundred feet later they come to a mammoth Western Red Cedar, next to a bench on which to sit and contemplate.

"The Ancient Cedar" is estimated at 500 years old, but Menashe says it's probably not the oldest tree on this trail. Altogether, only about 1 to 5 percent of old growth forest remains in the Puget Sound Basin, and Menashe says every bit of it is priceless and deserves to be saved.

. . .

DAN PEDERSEN

ABOUT THE AUTHOR

Dan Pedersen grew up in Western Washington and lived in Idaho in the 1970s while serving in the U.S. Air Force. He holds two journalism degrees from the University of Washington and worked as a reporter and editor for several newspapers in Idaho and Washington, including a large outdoor weekly. He is the author of nine books, many short stories and a weekly blog about nature and rural living, Dan's Blog. This is the fourth mystery in his Brad Haraldsen series.

Made in the USA
Las Vegas, NV
29 August 2021